How to Train Your Alpha

MM FARMER

HOW TO TRAIN YOUR ALPHA

Cover design by Erin Dameron-Hill (who is completely fabulous)

ASIN:

Paperback:

Click here for a complete list of other works by Merry Farmer.

If you'd like to be the first to learn about when the next books in the series come out and more, please sign up for my newsletter here: http://eepurl. com/RQ-KX

 Created with Vellum

Chapter One

Jesse

Of all the things I could have done with a long weekend right at the beginning of summer, attending the Bangers & Mash Emergency Support Alpha training program was not at the top of my list.

My mood had been off in a weird way from the moment I made the turn off the highway and started up the winding mountain road to the Mash Institute, the headquarters for the discreet, highly-regarded service. I couldn't make any sense of it as I parked in the lot down the hill from the collection of beautiful buildings that housed the program's classrooms and dormitories. It wasn't at all like me to go into an experience feeling...feeling.... I wasn't even sure what I was feeling. That was the odd part.

I was an alpha. I was usually confident and in control of my emotions. Maybe it was a little cliché, but I was always on top of things, always calm and in control. My job as a teacher at Olivarez High School demanded that I project an air of kind, fair authority at all times. Students needed that sort of guidance.

So why I felt like one of my own students, irritated and restless, as I shut my car door with a little too much force, clicked the keychain fob to lock it, then started along the pretty, landscaped path from the parking lot of the Mash Institute to the classroom building that was the centerpiece of the facility, I had no idea. If I didn't know better, I would have said it was a rush of adolescent hormones. But I was approaching thirty, for Christ's sake. I wasn't some kid.

My job as a high school teacher was, paradoxically, why I'd ended up being sent to the B&M training course to begin with. Olivarez High School was one of the finest secondary schools in Barrington, and we had a reputation for encouraging excellence in our omega students—something not every school could claim—and since I was the newest member of the teaching staff, Principal Winters had encouraged me to take the training course so that I might better understand our omega students.

Although why Winters thought it would be a good idea for me to learn all about how to service omegas in heat when the only ones I would normally be around were underage, years from their first heat, and definitely, *definitely* off-limits, was a mystery to me.

I hoisted my weekend bag over my shoulder, grumbling internally about wasting a perfectly good summer weekend taking classes I would never use when I could have been down by the beach, checking out omegas I might have a chance with. It wasn't the best attitude to have going into the experience, I knew, but it had been six months since things had ended between me and Greg, and I was finally ready to get back out there again.

More than that, the itch to find an omega to settle down

with had been nagging me for a while. Again, it was cliché, but now that I was settled in life with a solid job I loved, enough money in the bank to go looking for a house, and bright prospects for a future in education, marriage and family seemed like the next logical step.

I took the path from the parking lot to the classroom building with long strides, forcing myself not to scowl, not really interested in striking up a conversation with the other alphas heading into the building. My students always told me that, at over six feet and built like a tank, I looked intimidating as hell when I scowled, and I didn't want to take away from the training experience for my fellow classmates.

It was hard, though. Especially when I reached the door of the building, grabbed the handle to pull it open for a beta, then took one last look across the incredible vista from the mountain to the sparkling, blue water in the distance. Sunshine and sand would have to wait for another day.

My weirdly bad attitude took a hit the moment I stepped into the building. It was like entering another world. The entire Mash Institute was beautifully designed, with glass buildings that blended with the rugged mountain landscape and let in a ton of light. The walls of the classroom building were filled with beautiful abstract art and soothing colors. It was hard not to be in a good mood when faced with so much careful design and tranquility, but it almost felt like my emotions were being manipulated by the place.

Then again, every omega friend I'd ever had said that, when their heat hit, they felt like their emotions were being manipulated by biology. I remembered that and thought perhaps the decorations around me were a clever way to teach alphas empathy as I made my way to the registration desk at the other end of the lobby.

The place smelled amazing too, which just added to that disconcerting feeling of having my emotions controlled by something other than me. The air was filled with the sweet scent of everything from honeysuckle to chocolate icing to watermelon, which was a gigantic clue that it was packed full of omegas, and not underdeveloped, adolescent omegas, like I was used to. Normally, that much mature omega scent would have driven my libido crazy, but the intensity of it seemed to have the opposite effect, making me only low-level horny instead of pushing me into rut. It wasn't a half bad feeling, come to think of it.

Another thing my omega friends had always told me—when heat was approaching and they had an alpha they trusted or loved with them, being manipulated by emotion felt pretty damn good.

"Welcome to the Mash Institute," the beta behind the registration table greeted me as I approached. "Name?"

"Jesse Armstrong," I said, reminding myself to smile. The beta wasn't responsible for me losing a beach weekend, Winters was.

"Armstrong, Armstrong," the beta said, shuffling through a small tub of thick registration envelopes. "Ah, here we go." His face lit up a bit as he handed me the packet. "Congratulations on being selected for Mr. Mash's group. That's an accomplishment on top of an accomplishment."

"Really?" My brow inched up as I took the tag bearing my name from the paperclip around the envelope. "I'm just here to audit the course, not to become certified," I explained.

"Even better," the beta said. "For reasons that might be obvious, Mr. Mash is one of the best instructors we have."

"I guess it's my lucky day," I said, doubting that it was.

"Orientation is in fifteen minutes," the beta went on. "From there, you'll be taken up to your dormitory. All meals are communal in the dining hall, which is adjacent to this classroom building. Enjoy your stay, Mr. Armstrong."

"Thanks." I nodded and moved away to let the next alpha collect his training packet.

As I started across the lobby, following signs for my class group, I peeled the backing off my name-tag and stuck the tag to my shirt. I glanced around as I did. There were some good-looking guys standing around the lobby or heading down the corridor toward the classrooms. I'd never really been attracted to other alphas, but there was nothing wrong with a hot beta. Maybe I didn't need the beach to meet someone new. And if worse came to worst, maybe I could make it to the beach for half a day at the end of the weekend.

No, I thought, shaking my head at myself. The weekend was purely about continuing education now. Biology might have been pushing me to think of the future—and something about the Mash Institute was definitely highlighting that feeling—but the timing wasn't right. I had to focus on the classwork and what I could get out of it to help my students.

There were about two dozen other alphas wandering around the lobby, which seemed about right, according to everything I'd heard about the Bangers & Mash program. Obviously, way more alphas applied to the program than were accepted. Winters had explained to me that the screening process and training program for Emergency Support Alphas was stringent.

On the one hand, there were always those alphas who thought signing up for something like B&M would be an easy way to fuck as many omegas in heat as they could, guilt-free. On the other, assisting an omega through heat was a daunting task that took an alpha with a compassionate personality, not to mention incredible stamina. I'd never been with an omega in heat, but I heard it was draining. On top of that, from everything I'd been told, the turnover rate for Bangers & Mash alphas was incredibly high, because so many of them ended up either getting attached to a client and starting a real relationship with them, or they ended up exhausted and burnt out.

The relationships that had emerged from ESA servicing were probably why the top of the page on the application website for B&M stated in huge, bold letters, "THIS IS NOT A DATING SERVICE".

But you couldn't argue with the number of marriages that resulted from B&Ms services.

"How awesome is it that we were selected for the program?" a young alpha I didn't know asked me with a grin as he fell into step with me along the hall leading to the classroom.

I teetered between being unnaturally annoyed that someone wanted to make friends with me and just giving in and enjoying the experience for what it was for a moment. Then I let out a breath, dropped my shoulders, and smiled.

"I'm just auditing the class as professional development for my teaching job," I told the young guy as we stepped into classroom five. "But good on you for being accepted."

"Justin," the young alpha said, shuffling his class materials in his arms, then extending a hand to me. "And thanks."

"Jesse," I said as Justin read my name-tag, shaking his hand.

"I didn't know someone could just audit the class," Justin went on as we walked to the far side of the classroom, taking seats at a table bathed in sunlight. "I thought it was only for ESA trainees. Mind you, I didn't think I'd be accepted to the program on my first try," he zoomed on, speaking fast. "I'm only nineteen, and I'm on a gap year before college. My uncle knows Salazar Banger, though, and even though Mr. Banger told me in my interview that nepotism would never be a factor in who they allow into the program, I'm sure it counted for something. I just want to help people though, you know? And even though omegas have made incredible advances in the last generation, there is still far too much prejudice against them. I want to do my part."

I did my best not to chuckle at Justin's enthusiasm. He reminded me of my students. The ones we teachers had to watch out for, in case they were bullied by their far too cool classmates. Actually, Justin couldn't have been more than a couple years older than most of my students.

"Do you plan to pursue a career in omega support?" I asked as we sat and spread our class materials out over the table.

"I'm not sure yet," Justin said with an earnest look. "This gap year is supposed to help me decide what I want to do with the rest of my life. I think I would do well in some sort of service industry, though. I like helping people, and I feel drawn to omegas. Well," he added with a laugh, "what alpha doesn't, am I right?"

"True," I said with an indulgent grin, impatience still nagging me. Did Winters really need to send me here? For a whole weekend? Couldn't I have just read a book?

More students trickled in until there were eight of us at the tables. Justin continued talking about himself and his confused ambitions, almost going off into his own thoughts as he did. I was content just to let him talk until he exhausted himself. He probably needed someone to listen, like many of my students. I noted that most of the other alpha students arriving to sit at the other tables were around my age, though, in their late twenties. That seemed about right, since alphas hit their peak sexuality around thirty.

All the same, I still felt out of place, and every time I glanced out the window and caught a glimpse of the ocean glittering in the distance, I cursed Winters's name.

My attention was pulled away from the view of the ocean and my resentment of Winters, and Justin stopped his chattering, as two men entered the room, walking at a clip. One was an alpha who appeared to be in his early thirties, and the other was a slightly younger omega. I didn't sense any bond between them, and I almost didn't give either a second thought, until they headed to the front of the classroom instead of taking seats with the rest of the students.

"Good morning," the omega addressed us all from the front of the room, which threw me for another loop. He couldn't actually be— "I'm Phillip Mash, and I'll be your class instructor this weekend," he went on.

My brow shot up. I wasn't the only alpha in the class to have that reaction. Phillip Mash couldn't have been more than twenty-five, and he was gorgeous. He wasn't at all what I'd expected from an ESA training course.

"An omega is teaching the class?" Justin said by my side, voicing what I and probably every alpha in the class was thinking.

"This is my teaching assistant, Tybalt Martin, or Ty, as he likes to be called," Mash introduced the alpha with a friendly smile. Again, it was clear to me that they were friendly, but not bonded. "Welcome to Emergency Support Alpha training," Mash said, clasping his hands together.

I still hadn't recovered from my initial shock at having an omega for an instructor, but Mash had an air of authority about him that ran counter to what I thought I knew about omegas. He also had an edginess that I couldn't place. I couldn't figure out if I liked it or if it rubbed me the wrong way.

He was lithe and graceful, like most omegas I'd met, and his dark hair and large, dark eyes created exactly the kind of look that appealed to me. Maybe that was where my burst of unsettled emotion came from. I liked him at once, even though he made the strange sense of irritation I'd been feeling flare and growl. I didn't want to think about it too hard, but something about him made me hot, and my dick took notice.

I wrote off the attraction as biology and the excess of omega markers in the air, though. Winters had warned me that the energy at the Mash Institute was unusual because of everything that went on here.

"Yes, in case you were wondering," Mash went on, "my fathers are the founders of Bangers & Mash Emergency Support Alpha Services, Salazar Banger and Nicholas Mash.

"Just a little company history before we walk you through the itinerary of the next four days, then I'll let you head over to the dormitories to settle in before lunch," Mash continued. "My fathers founded B&M almost thirty years ago, after my papa's brother nearly died during a traumatic heat while he was working in a remote location. Uncle Lewis tried to tough it out on his own instead of putting himself at the mercy of an unknown and unfamiliar alpha. As you all know, the physical, mental, and emotional toll an omega endures during heat if he or she fails to find an alpha to knot them can be devastating, but the risk associated with engaging an unknown alpha to help us through heat can be even worse.

"After hearing the harrowing story of what Uncle Lewis went through," Mash continued, "and because Dad and Papa had several other friends who experienced traumatic heats, my fathers conceived the idea of creating a professional, responsible, trusted service of thoroughly vetted alphas, skilled at taking omegas through their heat. They wanted to provide unattached omegas with compassionate, safe alpha care without any risk of unwanted pregnancy or families with more conservative viewpoints demanding that omegas marry the alphas who took their heat.

"B&M is a discreet service, and one of the very first rules all of you must adhere to is strict confidentiality when it comes to the omega clients you are sent to assist," Mash said. "Some of our clients require absolute secrecy, due to their family or life circumstances. Many of them request the same alpha for every heat, because they know they can rely on you. We do not advertise our services publicly, but the existence and reputation of Bangers & Mash has spread by word of mouth, which is why we have open applications for alphas and hold regular training sessions like these.

"In the next four days, you will learn not only the basics of omega biology and the process and needs of heat, you will learn the B&M heat protocol, which must be observed during every call you may be sent on. This includes different methods of contraception and how to use them, our tried and tested procedure for initiating a heat encounter, and the steps and considerations you must adhere to when engaged with an omega who has called on our services. You are here to serve omegas, gentlemen, not yourselves."

In spite of the fact that I had no intention of ever taking advantage of an omega—I had no intention of actually becoming an ESA at all—something about the way Mash practically scolded the class with those words had me hot under the collar. Omegas had been dealing with prejudice for centuries, true, but there was just as much prejudice against us alphas. We were not all sex-starved beasts who couldn't control ourselves in the presence of an omega, even one approaching heat. Hell, I had a hard time imagining an alpha like Justin so much as saying boo to an omega like Phillip Mash.

Or maybe it was just something about Phillip Mash that set me off. I had to admit, I had a visceral reaction to the man. I could smell him across the room, like fresh peaches and cream. Every omega had his own scent—always sweet, always delicious—but I'd rarely met one whose scent tickled my sweet-tooth quite the way Mash's did.

It was annoying. Beyond annoying. It got under my skin and made me restless in a way I usually wasn't. Mash was my teacher, and as I well knew, attraction between teachers and students was the most forbidden kind of taboo. You just didn't go there if you wanted to keep your job, your reputation, and your freedom.

"Do you have something you'd like to add or ask?" Mash said with a touch of impatience in his voice.

It took me a hot second to realize he was addressing me. The way he looked at me...I didn't know what it was, but it got under my skin.

"I'm just auditing the class," I said, sitting back in my chair and crossing my arms. "I doubt I'll have any questions."

A look of understanding dawned in Mash's expression. It was almost cocky.

It set my teeth on edge for some reason.

"Ah, you must be Mr. Armstrong," Mash said, color splashing his cheeks, almost like someone had warned him about me. Which made no sense, since there was nothing remarkable about me at all. "James Winters requested that my father included you in my group. I don't usually accept auditors."

"I don't usually audit classes over long weekends when I could be at the beach," I snapped in reply.

A few of the other trainees laughed nervously. Mash's eyes went wide. Honestly, I was a little shocked at myself. I was acting like a hormonal teenager in one of my classes—the kind who gave me a headache.

It had to be the atmosphere of the institute.

"I'm so sorry to be ruining your weekend, Mr. Armstrong," Mash ground out. "But since the rest of the gentlemen here have gone through a great deal to be selected for this program, and since the training I intend to carry out over the next few days could very well protect the life and sanity of your omega friends and neighbors, I would ask that you keep an open mind...and a closed mouth."

I bristled, but not with anger. I was completely in the wrong, and I felt like an ass.

That didn't stop the way Mash hit all my nerves, though.

"I'm sorry," I said, arms still crossed tightly. "I don't mean to be such an ass."

Mash seemed to ease up by a hair as well. He addressed the class as a whole when he said, "You may notice that the intensity of both alpha and omega pheromones concentrated around the institute is higher than what you are used to in society at large. Because alphas and omegas only make up twenty percent of the general population each, most people don't experience such intense concentrations in everyday life. In addition, about a third of our omega clients choose to spend their heats with an ESA in one of our secluded mountain cabins, which means the pheromones are even more intense in most places on the mountain. It's why our institute was constructed away from the center of Barrington and its suburbs."

Mash looked right at me as he said, "Different people experience different reactions to the intensity of pheromones."

That definitely explained it, but it didn't make me feel better.

I clenched my jaw and kept my mouth shut, like Mash had ordered me to, but my eyes never left him as he turned to walk over to a smartboard at the front of the classroom.

"I'm sure you have questions," he said, "but let me just run through a brief presentation first, then I'll give you time to ask them."

I was sure he would. I felt like I had a million questions after all, but none of them coalesced into thoughts or words.

The only thought that felt clear to me as Mash turned to tap the smartboard to start his presentation was that the cocky omega had a perfect ass.

Chapter Two

Phillip

Cedar wood after a fresh rain. That was the scent that I couldn't get out of my nose as I ran through the schedule for ESA training over the next few days with the latest batch of alpha recruits. The scent filled me with a deep sense of calm, and of childhood memories of camping with my father, brothers, and sister.

At the same time, it annoyed the crap out of me. The last thing I needed when I had a class to teach and a job to do was an alpha scent that powerful muddling my thoughts and emotions. I was around alphas all the time in my job at the institute. I'd *thought* I'd reached the point where I could tune out alpha markers.

So much for that idea.

"The training course consists of two parts," I said, focusing on the smartboard as I called up information and graphics to illustrate the various units of the course. "This afternoon and tomorrow morning, we'll work on omega and alpha biology, both individually and as they relate to each other."

"Sounds like what I teach high school kids," Armstrong said, just barely loud enough for me to hear.

I paused in the middle of switching to another slide, pursed my lips, and stared flatly at Armstrong. "Do you have something to add?" I asked, working hard not to sound unnecessarily peevish and failing.

Armstrong looked surprised. He still had his thick, muscled arms crossed, but his brow flew up in surprise. "No, sir," he said, sounding as puzzled as he looked.

My shoulders bunched slightly with an awkward combination of embarrassment and frustration. Maybe I'd been imagining things.

I nodded to Armstrong, then turned back to the board. "Male omega biology and female omega biology have distinct differences, which we will discuss," I went on, pushing aside my strange, unsettled feelings. "And contrary to popular myths that keep being perpetuated, male omega anatomy is not simply female organs manifested in a male body. Omegas are not just male women. There are many, many nuances that make male omegas very different than female omegas or betas."

I must have been harder up for alpha companionship than I'd thought if I was imagining an alpha like Armstrong talking back to me. True, my heat was coming sometime in the next week. I had more than enough time to teach the class before I would need to retreat to my cabin at the very top of the mountain with Ty, or whichever of my other ESAs friends had three or four days to spare for a heat. My pheromone levels were higher than usual before a heat, but not so much as to be noteworthy.

"After we've discussed omega biology," I went on, clicking

to another slide, "we'll spend a bit of time on alpha biology, which I'm certain you're all very familiar with."

A few of the alpha students chuckled. My gaze shot straight to Armstrong to see if he was one of them.

The man's expression was neutral, but I felt antagonism pouring off of him, like he wanted to pick a fight or question what right an omega had to teach about alpha biology.

No, it wasn't antagonism, exactly. It was more like...aggression, command. Like he wanted to grab me, bend me over the desk, and have his way with me.

And I might actually like it.

I cleared my throat and tried to focus. It wasn't me; it was biology. Armstrong had all the classic markers of a particularly virile alpha. He was tall, with broad shoulders and well-defined muscles. His square jaw was clean-shaven, but even at mid-morning, stubble was beginning to show. Additionally, Armstrong had the high cheekbones, blue eyes, and sandy-blond hair that was considered to be particularly attractive to most omegas.

Alright, I was willing to admit it was attractive to me too. I could objectively say that Armstrong was smoking hot. And I would concede that I had a natural reaction to the man. But I'd reacted to alphas before. It was just one of the things about the omega body I'd been born with that pissed me off, just like my beta sister constantly complained about PMS mood swings and cramps.

"We'll finish up the morning tomorrow with a unit on omega and alpha psychology," I went on, a little too aware that I'd paused for a moment to gather my scattering thoughts. "Then we'll move on to spend tomorrow afternoon discussing contraceptives and their use."

Because heaven only knew that not every omega out there wanted to spend their life as a brood mare for an alpha, whether they were in a loving relationship or not. I certainly didn't want to be tied down in a life where I would be nothing more than a parent raising child after child. That was the life my papa had wanted, but I wasn't Papa.

Just as I clicked the slides over and went on to talk about day three and some of the practical training they would engage in, there was a knock at the classroom door. As if my thoughts had summoned him, Papa popped his head into the room.

"Sorry to interrupt," Papa said. "Phillip, can I speak to you for a moment?"

A niggle of dread hit my gut. For some ungodly reason, I glanced straight to Armstrong. The scent of cedar and rain hit me again, and this time, I felt a surge with it, like my body was gearing up to generate a massive slick that would leave me needing to change my trousers.

As if I needed anything else to embarrass me in front of my class.

"Sure, Papa," I said, glancing to Ty. "Could you take over for me for a second?"

"Absolutely," Ty said with a nod.

I stepped away from the front of the room. "I'll be right back," I told the class.

Again, I looked straight at Armstrong as I did, but only for a moment before forcing myself to look away. I had a bad feeling the scent that tickled my nose belonged to Armstrong, and if it did, I was in for a rough next couple of days.

"Did you need something?" I asked Papa once we were in the hall.

It wasn't a good sign that my alpha dad was there too. On his own, I never worried about Papa. Papa was an omega like me, and for whatever reason, the two of us had a relationship that made us feel like brothers half the time.

Dad was another story. I loved him like crazy—like I did my entire family—but when Dad had that firm, alpha look in his eyes, I felt like I was a kid again, waiting to be told off.

Sure enough, Dad crossed his arms, his brow knit with concern, and asked, "What's this your papa tells me about you wanting to quit teaching?"

I swallowed hard. I'd known this conversation was coming, but like anything unpleasant, I'd hoped to avoid it as long as possible.

"I don't want to quit entirely, Dad," I said, crossing my arms in imitation of him—and thinking of Armstrong as I did —then darting a quick look to Papa. "I love teaching, you know I do. And I'm passionate about the work we do here at Bangers & Mash."

"But?" Dad said in a leading tone.

I sighed. There was no point in delaying anymore, even though I knew what both Dad and Papa would say about it. "But I've been doing this for a few years now, ever since getting my degree, and I...I feel like it's time for a change. I want to try something else. Maybe travel. I just feel so...restless, like something is waiting for me and I need to go after it, something new."

Dad and Papa exchanged a look. They both grinned, like they knew more than me. I liked seeing the two of them when they were like that, actually. After nearly thirty-five years of marriage and five kids, they were as much in love as ever. Papa had had his last heat years ago, but I knew for a fact—though I wished I didn't—that the two of them were just as wild with each other in bed as they had been when they'd first met on a singles' cruise.

"Something new," Dad repeated my statement. His lips twitched with mirth as he asked, "Like what?"

I had no patience for where I knew he was going with the question. "I am not looking to get married and have kids, Dad, Papa." I frowned at both of them. "Just because I'm an omega does not mean I have some stupid biological time-bomb ticking away in me that can only be satisfied if I get pregnant.

17

Plenty of omegas these days never have children, and they go on to live useful, fulfilling lives. And before you say it, I don't need an alpha mate to feel like I'm living a good life. I just feel, like, I don't know. Like I want to try something different, see what's out there in the world."

Dad and Papa exchanged another look, even closer to laughing than they'd been before.

"Neither of us said anything about alphas or children, Philly," Papa said, too much of a twinkle in his eyes.

My face heated. I felt like I'd botched an interview, even though they would have brought up the whole alpha and children thing eventually.

"What do you want to do?" Dad asked. "Travel? Head out west to Uncle Xavier's ranch maybe? Get a job as a long-shoreman?"

That last one was an obvious joke, and I did not appreciate it. I scowled at Dad, narrowing my eyes. While omegas weren't forbidden from joining whatever profession they wanted these days, like they had been in my grandfathers' time, the idea of an omega as a longshoreman was laughable, even to me. The job was too physical for most omegas' capabilities, for one, and if an omega went into heat in a situation like that, it could disrupt everyone on the boat.

"I haven't thought about what I want to do yet," I said, "but I have a few ideas. Nothing that jumps out yet, though, I'm just restless, thinking about it. But for the time being," I went on, cutting off what looked like another question from Dad, "can I please finish teaching this class? Then I'd like to take a break, regroup, and figure out what I want to do next. Is that too much to ask?"

"No, not at all," Papa said, resting a hand on my shoulder and smiling. "You take all the time you need, honey." He peeked at Dad, as though he already knew the conclusion I'd come to about life after taking that time.

Dad just nodded. "What do you think of the new class of recruits?" he asked.

"Orientation has only just started," I said. "I haven't had time to assess them individually. They all seem nice." Except for the one who had gotten under my skin and in my nose, messing up my usual flow.

"Let me know if Justin Mallow is a problem," Dad said. "He's the nephew of a friend, and I know we don't usually take alphas that young, but when I interviewed him, I found him to be an exceptional young man."

"I'll let you know," I said. I started to turn back to the classroom, but paused. A huge part of me didn't want to open the can of worms right in front of me, but I had to ask. "Are the scent dampeners in the building malfunctioning today?"

Dad frowned and Papa shrugged. "I don't think so," Papa said. "Why?"

I shook my head. "No reason. It's just that some of my class seems a little edgy this time."

"Edgy, huh?" Dad asked, that annoying, father-knows-best grin back in his eyes. "Your class?"

"It's nothing," I said, knowing what he was implying and shrugging it off. "I've got a class to teach. Will the two of you be around for lunch?"

"Of course," Papa said with a smile. "We have to give our introductory speech."

I wanted to roll my eyes. Papa thought he was some sort of comedian when it came to the welcoming speech he and Dad did with each new training class. Dad went along with it, and yeah, the students who came to train as ESAs usually thought they were hilarious, but my siblings and I had never seen anything remotely funny about their antics.

Dad thumped my arm and gave me a fatherly wink. "Do good in there, son," he told me in that way he had that made

19

me glow with self-confidence. "You're doing important work. We all are."

"Thanks, Dad."

I headed back into the classroom with a smile, bolstered for the time being. They might question my decisions and give me a hard time, but Dad and Papa were understanding when it came to letting their children do what they wanted with their lives.

My warm and fuzzy feeling immediately crackled into an entirely different sort of warmth as I stepped back into the classroom. For some reason, the scent of cedar had doubled in my absence. Again, my gaze darted straight to Armstrong, even though I told myself repeatedly not to look at him. I flat out rejected the soft feeling of slick that filled my ass as I walked back to the front of the room.

"And we'll end the weekend with a mock omega call for each of you," Ty was just finishing up the orientation spiel. "That will serve as your final exam, so to speak. After that, you'll be certified." He nodded to me as I resumed my place at the front of the classroom.

"Sounds like you covered everything," I said, forcing my shoulders to drop and a smile to grace my face.

"More or less," Ty said, stepping back and gesturing for me to resume my spot.

Ty was a good guy and an experienced ESA. One of the best we had. He was alpha to the core, but he had a deep respect for omegas, and for my Dad and Papa. He was also one of the most in-demand alphas B&M employed, which could have had something to do with his astounding good looks and sculpted body.

I checked the smartboard to make sure I knew where we were in the presentation, then faced the class again. "So, any questions?" I asked. One of the alphas whose name I hadn't learned yet raised his hand. I squinted at his name-tag, then said, "Mason?"

The alpha lowered his hand and asked, "What happens if we fail the course?"

"It isn't a course you can pass or fail," I explained. "Although if I or Ty or any of the assessors at the end of the weekend feel you aren't a good fit for B&M after all, at least you'll be able to say you learned a few valuable skills that will help you with your future partner."

"You mean we might be rejected as an ESA, even after this weekend?" Justin asked, eyes wide with horror.

"Not rejected, no," I clarified, a bit hesitant. "B&M has various tiers of ESAs that are more suited toward omegas with different needs and personalities. Ninety-nine percent of our graduates are given a classification that will ensure they're matched up with compatible omegas, when the time comes."

"What if there's a mismatch?" Armstrong asked without raising his hand. "How do you handle it if an alpha shows up to a call and he and the omega don't get along?"

The question set my teeth on edge, but I couldn't figure out why.

"I thought you were just auditing and that you wouldn't ask any questions, Mr. Armstrong," I said, trying to channel a little of Papa's energy by teasing the man.

My efforts flopped. Armstrong stared flatly back at me. "I think it's a legitimate question."

I smiled tightly, caught between wanting to apologize—which was not like me at all—and to ask the alpha who he thought he was.

"As far as I know," I said, "there has never been an incident where the alpha sent by B&M and the omega he's been called to service have gotten along so badly that the call was canceled. In most cases, by the time an omega places a call for an ESA, he or she is in such dire circumstances that nature takes over and they just get on with things. As I believe we've stressed several times so far, and will continue to stress, the point of this training course is to produce alphas who operate under rules of exceptional professionalism. If the pairing isn't the best match, the omega won't ask for that particular alpha to assist with their next heat."

Armstrong nodded. I couldn't tell if his reaction was adversarial or if I'd answered his question adequately. Something about him still rubbed me the wrong way.

Or maybe it wasn't the wrong way. Maybe Armstrong rubbed me the right way, only at the wrong time. Papa would probably tease me about it later and tell me it was a bad idea to teach a class so close to a heat. At least I could use that as an argument in favor of Dad and Papa letting me take a sabbatical to go off and try something else.

Either way, the one thing I was sure of was that I wasn't going to let my visceral reaction to some random alpha student affect my class or my life. Jesse Armstrong would only be at the Mash Institute for four days. Once he was gone, I might not ever have to see him again, which would be fine, as far as I was concerned.

Or was it? The thought of not seeing him again, even though I'd only just met him, felt like a rock in my gut.

"If there are no more questions," I said, feigning ease and affability, "I'll leave you all to take your things to the dormitory and to find your assigned rooms. Then I'll meet you in the dining hall for lunch."

The room erupted into the scrape of chairs and the shuffle of alphas as they got up and gathered their things. Justin leaned over to say something to Armstrong. I could have sworn I heard Armstrong reply with, "I just hope I can make it through the weekend in one piece and then get to the beach."

When I glanced back to him as I crossed to the desk to

pick up my own things, his mouth wasn't moving, and he was thoroughly distracted by whatever Justin was saying.

A hot shiver shot down my spine. I was imagining things again.

At least, I hoped I was imagining things. It was rare, but there was another reason I might have heard Armstrong speak across the distance of the classroom, why I might catch his scent above everyone else's, and why I was reacting so strongly to him. A reason I definitely didn't want to think about.

Chapter Three

Jesse

One day of ESA training classes, and I was pretty sure I would never have cut it as a service alpha. I usually had more patience than I'd had sitting through Mash's lectures on biology and psychology. The rest of the class was fascinated by the deep dive into both subjects that Mash gave us. It was way more than I'd ever been taught about omega biology in college, that much was certain.

Maybe it was the blunt way Mash talked about the physical changes that omegas went through when they were in heat—the relaxation and dilation of muscles in their asses, the opening of the passage leading to their wombs and the closing of their rectums so that alpha ejaculate made it to the right place, and the series of nerves and glands along the breeding passage that brought omegas insane levels of pleasure and multiple, continuous orgasms when an alpha was inside of them during heat. If I'd been teaching the same things to my high school students, the class would have dissolved into embarrassed, horny giggles right from the start.

Mash delivered all the information as if he were teaching driver's ed at the DMV. I don't know why it annoyed me. But then, I'd stopped puzzling over the reaction I had to Phillip Mash sometime halfway through the first session after lunch. He just got to me. There was no getting around it. I had a hard time listening to Mash discussing an omega's increased output of slick during heat or following his words as he walked us through a larger-than-life diagram of internal omega anatomy.

Or, really, if I was honest with myself, I should have said that I had a hard time listening to Mash talk bluntly about such personal, borderline taboo, subjects without imagining he was an omega in heat, reduced to wearing specially designed undergarments to catch his slick and prevent embarrassment, smelling like a dream, his asshole dilated and begging to be filled.

"Jesse? Jesse? Are you okay?"

The question, delivered with a teasing grin by Justin as a group of us from class sat around one of the cafeteria tables for supper felt more like Justin had poured a glass of ice water down my back.

"Yeah, I was just thinking about some of the things we learned in class today," I said, telling the truth, but making it sound inconsequential.

Ryland, one of the other alphas, who sat across from me, laughed ironically. He shook his head as he cut the exquisite steak we'd been served for supper. "I won't say it was too much information, because we're going to need to know all of that when we're in a heat situation with a client, but it was a lot." His eyes went wide at the end of the sentence.

"I didn't know half the stuff we discussed today," Justin said, leafing through his training manual as he ate. "Like, no one ever told me omegas have such sensitive breeding passages."

"No one talked about omegas or heat or any of that for generations," Ben, one of the other alphas I'd met that afternoon, said with a shrug. "But like Mr. Mash said, making all of that some sort of big secret was just another archaic way of thinking that used to relegate omegas to an inferior status in society."

"It's funny," Ryland laughed, chewed a bite of his steak, then swallowed and went on. "Back in the nineteenth century, people used to think most women weren't remotely interested in sex, and that most omegas couldn't think about anything *but* sex, so both were kept away from men and alphas."

"I'm glad we all got over those stupid viewpoints," Justin said, shutting his training manual and focusing on his food. "Personally, I love omegas. I always have. I just like being around them. I had an omega teacher for second grade, Mr. Klinger, and I used to follow him around like a puppy."

"That doesn't surprise me at all," I said, grinning at Justin.

Justin smiled in return, realizing I was just teasing him, fortunately.

If I had left it there, everything would have been fine. But the feeling of restlessness and impatience that had plagued me all day loosened my tongue a little too much.

"I can understand why our great-grandparents felt that way about omegas, though," I said, speaking a little too loudly. "It's distracting for alphas to have omegas in heat wandering around. Even when they're masking their scent or dimming their other omega markers. It's just a fact of nature that omegas affect alphas when they're in heat. And yes, it's our responsibility to rein it in and keep ourselves in check. I'm not one of those conservative nuts who thinks an omega is responsible for being attacked by an alpha because they were wearing revealing clothes or not hiding their scent, but—"

"But what, Mr. Armstrong?"

The question that came from behind me was like someone ringing a gong and shattering it right next to my ear. I knew I shouldn't have spoken so loudly and that I should have kept my opinions to myself.

I twisted gingerly in my chair to find Phillip Mash right behind me, holding a plate and a drink, as if he were on his way to a table to eat. The aroma of steak and garlic wasn't enough to mask the peaches and cream scent that wafted off him like a waterfall. Even with a scowl, his refined, dark features and large eyes went straight to my gut. No, not my gut, a little lower.

"What do you think an omega's responsibility to mask themselves while they're in heat is, Mr. Armstrong?" Mash asked, as firm as iron.

I ignored the fact that I was close to being as firm as iron myself and cleared my throat.

"I'm sorry," I said, doubling the amount of respect I would usually show a fellow teacher, not to mention an omega. "I didn't mean to imply that an omega has any obligation to look or behave a certain way for the sake of alphas."

Mash almost looked satisfied, but I had to go ahead and add, "But you have to admit that biology is biology, and alphas are programmed to respond to omegas in heat."

The corner of Mash's mouth twitched, probably in disapproval. He stood almost perfectly still for a moment, but I could have sworn I could see the blood moving under his skin. Skin that was starting to glow pink, I noticed. Like he had a sunburn or had run a marathon and only just rested before cooling down.

It hit me then. Mash was nearing a heat. We'd just learned about all of the markers in class—a class taught by him—not more than two hours before. His scent was strong, his skin was flushed, and if I touched him, he'd probably be warm, and his pupils were just a little bit dilated. Of course, that instantly had me wondering if he was wet and if his asshole was twitching as the muscles got ready to stretch wide.

As soon as my body reacted to those thoughts, going hard in all the right places at the wrong time, I pushed the notion away. I had heat on the brain after class. There was no way that the Mash Institute would let an omega who was anywhere near his heat teach in a room full of alphas. No, it was not Mash's responsibility to mask his markers so that a room full of alphas would keep their dicks in their pants, but like I'd argued before, biology was biology, and everything I'd learned about Phillip Mash so far told me that he was far too intelligent to put himself in that sort of situation.

Mash studied me for a long time, radiating irritation along with scent and heat. Then he heaved a sigh, leaned toward the table, and set his plate and cup down.

"Come with me, Mr. Armstrong," he said. "I have something I want to show you."

Surprised, I just blinked at him for a second. When he stepped back from the table, I stood, confused and self-conscious. It didn't help matters that Justin, Ryland, and Ben made the exact same sounds that my students did when one of them got in trouble and was called to the principal's office.

"Everything alright, Phil?" the senior Mr. Mash said from one of the tables we passed as Mash led me toward the dining room door.

"Just showing one of my students some family history, Papa," Mash replied. "We'll be back before dessert."

"Mr. Mash, Mr. Banger," I said, nodding toward the institute's founders as I followed the younger Mash.

"Let us know if you need anything," Mr. Banger called out as we headed for the door.

"Will do, Dad," Mash said before pushing open the door and holding it for me.

I considered myself a modern-thinking alpha, but having an omega like Mash hold the door for me just added to my oversensitive feelings of wrongness. He wasn't just an omega with a gorgeous face and an even more spectacular ass who had my blood pumping as soon as the breeze blowing across the mountain wafted his scent to me as we stepped outside, he was my teacher, the son of the men who had founded Bangers & Mash, and someone who deserved my respect.

I liked him, I realized as we headed out the door. He was the kind of guy I would have engaged in conversation if we'd met at a bar or on the beach. I was intrigued by what he did for a living and curious about what else he enjoyed in life. Yes, something about Mash irritated me, but something even bigger drew me toward him.

The man raised too many conflicting emotions in me—which seemed to be reflected in the weather and the hint of rain in the air—and even though I had no idea where we were going as we followed a smaller, dirt path away from the main buildings of the complex and on toward a bridge spanning a deep ravine, I said nothing. I didn't trust myself not to open my mouth and stick my foot in it again.

Mash evidently wasn't in a mood for chit-chat either. We walked along the mountain path in silence. The whole place was one spectacular view after another, all of them shrouded in twilight and an impending storm now. I glanced off to the ocean in the distance at one point and was surprised that I didn't feel the same pang of disappointment or resentment that I had before. That could have been because clouds had moved in and the scent of rain was in the air. But beyond that, I felt like I was exactly where I needed to be, which was yet another frustrating shift of emotions that felt like it was coming from outside of me.

I figured out which part of the Mash Institute's complex we were in, even though I hadn't been up there yet, as we walked past several secluded cabins. This must have been the part of the complex where omegas came when they wanted to have their heat serviced in private, outside of their everyday lives. Just knowing that any number of the cabins around us could have been occupied by mating couples kicked my libido up another notch that I didn't need.

By the time we crossed another bridge to an even more private-looking part of the mountain, I was ready to grab Mash by the shoulders to stop him and to spin him around so I could demand he tell me where we were going. The only thing that stopped me from accusing him of taking me somewhere he could throw me off the mountain to get rid of me was the small cabin tucked against the side of the mountain that we were clearly heading toward. The cabin looked less generic than the others and slightly more lived in.

"It's easy for alphas to joke about omegas in heat and to throw their opinions around," Mash finally started speaking as he fished a set of keys from his pocket, "but I doubt you'd be so glib if you knew what we've gone through, even in more recent generations, since omega acceptance has become the norm."

"I didn't mean to make it sound like I thought we should go back to omega compounds and brothels," I said, following Mash into the cabin with a scowl. "I definitely don't. I think B&M was a brilliant idea and that it helps omegas in a real, tangible way." It was just that my head was telling me one, sensible thing, and every other part of my body and gut was roaring something else at me.

Mash sent me a doubting look over his shoulder, set his keys on an end table next to a small sofa in the living room right on the other side of the cabin door, and walked straight to a desk that sat in one corner of the room. The desk had a computer and was covered with neatly arranged paperwork. That combined with the family pictures on the wall, the shelf full of books, and a glimpse of a kitchen through a wide doorway off to one side, made it clear that Mash lived in this cottage.

I tried not to speculate about the bedroom I could see through an open door on the other side of the room. Mash's scent was all over the cabin, but it seemed particularly acute in the bedroom. It had my mouth watering, my heart racing, and my dick filling.

Mash crossed to the bookshelf and selected a particularly old-looking book from a top shelf. As he did, a rumble of thunder sounded outside. It was a little too perfect, like someone had scored a movie where something bad was about to happen. I didn't know whether to laugh or shiver.

"This little piece of family history has been handed down on my Papa's side for generations," Mash said, completely serious as he opened the old tome and brought it over to me. "If you think what unattached omegas had to endure in the past is something to laugh about or a reason to demand all omegas marry before their first heat, maybe this will change your mind."

"I never said I agreed with those old laws ordering omegas to marry," I said, frowning, as Mash handed the book to me.

The marriage laws of a hundred years ago were some idiot's idea of compassionate progress and kindness toward omegas, but more often than not, they'd led to matches that more or less counted as child marriage, and usually the omega ended up married to whatever alpha stranger the family could find on short notice and pay to wed their sons and daughters, since first heats sometimes came as a surprise. There were well-known cases of crooked alphas who had illegally married up to twenty omegas, taken their first heats, then left them destitute and pregnant.

I had a feeling the book Mash wanted to show me was something along those lines. As raindrops began to hit the windowpanes, I took the book and stared at it. It was actually a ledger. It looked more like a register for a hotel, documenting guest names, how long they'd stayed, and how much they'd paid for those nights. But instead of room numbers, there were names at the top of each page.

My stomach turned a little as I realized what I was looking at.

"Is this a record book for an omega brothel?" I asked.

Mash nodded. "It is," he said. "The one my great-grandfather, Frederick Mash, was forced to go to work for when his first heat caught him unprepared."

I frowned. "Was this back when the law forced omegas to marry before their first heat?"

"Yes. What people don't like to talk about these days is the fact that if an omega couldn't find an alpha willing to marry him, they were sent to private brothels like these," Mash explained.

"And the law allowed that?" I asked, the sense of dread in my gut growing.

Mash laughed and shook his head. "Allowed it? It *was* the law, Mr. Armstrong. My great-grandfather Frederick's family tried to keep his heat a secret. They tried to hide him, but one of his teachers alerted the authorities. The police came and took him away without giving him any time to pack a bag or say goodbye to his brothers and sisters. He was barely eighteen."

I closed the ledger respectfully, and Mash took it back from me.

"Great-Grandfather Frederick came back from his stay at the brothel pregnant with my grandfather two years after that first heat," Mash said. "He didn't know who the father was, because the unscrupulous owner of that particular brothel sent a different alpha into the room for each heat wave, not just for the three or four days that a heat lasts."

I recoiled at that. Having more than one alpha for a heat was considered offensive in the extreme. Not a single omega I knew would have dreamed of such a thing. The fact that young men, and women too, I assumed, were subjected to something so shocking made everything Mash was telling me so much worse.

"And my grandfather wasn't Great-Grandfather Frederick's first pregnancy either," Mash went on. "The brothel reported the others as miscarriages, but the ledger shows that my great-grandfather was a popular commodity. He was certain that hellhole gave him something to cause the miscarriages. The brothel only let him go when he stopped being so fresh and popular."

"I'm so sorry you have that in your family history," I told him, meaning it genuinely.

I growled the words, though. Almost like I didn't mean them at all. Something wasn't right about that. I felt terrible for the injustices omegas had endured throughout history, but my jaw was clenched anyhow, I couldn't seem to take a deep, relaxed breath, and the restlessness I had felt all day had me ready to come out of my skin.

Again, as if someone had scored the scene perfectly, lightning flashed, and thunder rumbled outside a moment later. The rain against the windows picked up as the storm moved in.

"Those laws and the brothels were eradicated fifty years ago," Mash went on, determined to continue with his explanation, "but the attitudes toward omegas still exist in a lot of places."

He took the book back to the shelf, but I noticed that he nearly dropped it as he lifted it to the higher shelf when another flash of lightning and roll of thunder sounded. He seemed to fumble the large book even once he got it on the shelf.

I sucked in a breath. Clumsiness was another of the smaller signs of heat we'd learned about in class that morning. So was alpha aggression when secluded with an omega about to go into heat, come to think of it.

"My fathers didn't just start Bangers & Mash because of Uncle Lewis," Mash said as he turned and walked back to me. His face was flushed, and whether he was aware of it or not, he reached up to unbutton the top two buttons of his shirt, as if he were boiling hot. "They started the service in honor of my great-grandfather and all those omegas who were forced into sex work simply because of their biology. They started it so that omegas wouldn't have to marry strangers and bear their children, whether they wanted to or not. The hallmark of B&M is discretion. It's nobody's business who an omega calls on to take them through their heat, whether they want to marry them or not, and especially whether they want to have children. We are here to—"

His words stopped as he walked back toward me and nearly stumbled and fell along the way.

"Whoa!" I rushed forward and caught him before he spilled to the carpet, just as another crack of thunder sounded. It was so close to us that the hair stood up on the back of my neck. Or maybe that jolt of energy was from the contact the bare skin of my hands and wrists had with his hands. "Are you okay?"

Mash groaned, his weight sagging into me. "No, I don't think I am," he said, his voice plaintive and desperate. "Fuck. It's too early," he went on. "I still have a week. I swear, I still have a week."

"No, you don't," I said, a burst of authority and certainty filling me. As soon as I stopped fighting the truth and alpha nature, everything became crystal clear. Or maybe it had something to do with the touch of skin on skin that sent pulses of rightness through me. "The signs are all there, Mr.

Mash. Your scent is overpowering, you're burning hot to the touch, you're getting clumsy, and if I had to guess, I'd say you're getting pretty uncomfortable." That was the gentlest way I could think of to suggest his ass was open and throbbing and that he was leaking slick like it was going out of style.

Mash groaned again and tried to steady himself on his own feet. "I think you'd better call me Phillip," he said, having a hard time catching his breath.

"Yeah, and it's Jesse, not Mr. Armstrong," I said.

Phillip nodded, and started slowly toward the cabin door. "Ty said he'd help me through this heat. If we can just get back to the dining hall, I can—"

Phillip was cut off by a crash of thunder, but also by a powerful cramp that had him doubling over and nearly falling again.

I caught him for a second time, but this time I tugged him firmly into my arms. If he was cramping that badly, there was no time for him to go anywhere. He would spend the next three or four days in excruciating pain if he didn't have an alpha to fuck him and knot him through the whole thing.

"Why don't you wait here, Phillip," I said, steering him toward the sofa. "I can head back to the dining hall and get Ty to—"

This time, I was cut off by a crack of thunder that felt like it was right outside the cabin. Worse than that, as soon as the rumble stopped, there was a different sort of crack, like something splintering, then a thudding crash as something fell over.

"That sounded like a tree," Phillip said as I led him to the sofa and helped him to lie down.

"Yeah, it did," I said.

As soon as Phillip was settled, I left him and ran to the window. What I saw was like a punch in the gut.

"Uh, Phillip?" I asked, gaping out the window. "Is there

another way to get to the dining hall other than crossing that bridge we came across earlier?"

"No," Phillip groaned. "Why?"

I laughed humorlessly. "That tree you just heard fall landed on the bridge and obliterated it. We're trapped here."

Chapter Four

Phillip

There was no way it was actually happening. It couldn't be. Not only was it too early for me to go into heat, I was deeply unamused by the fact that I was trapped with an alpha I barely knew—a student at that—in an emergency situation. I didn't even like Jesse Armstrong.

No, that wasn't true. I barely knew Jesse. Yes, I'd had a reaction to the man from the moment I'd stepped into the classroom and seen him, but there was nothing unusual about having a reaction to an alpha, especially when I was so close to—

My thoughts ended abruptly as a heat cramp hit me, and I grunted, gripping my middle and crunching into a ball on the sofa.

This definitely wasn't happening.

Except it was.

"I could go out and check to see if it's just a trick of the light," Jesse said, still standing at the window, peering out into the darkness. His voice sounded grim as he went on with, "I think it's really gone, though. That tree fell right through it."

I knew what that meant, but I fought it the same way I fought the pain from the cramp. As soon as it eased up enough for me to speak, I said, "Let me call down to my dad to see if they can, I don't know, put up a temporary bridge to get Ty up here."

Jesse peeled away from the window and nodded. "Sounds good. Where's your phone?"

Jesse had an entirely different air about him all of a sudden. All day, he'd been annoying the hell out of me with his attitude, like he was resisting every word that came out of my mouth just because I was an omega and he was an alpha. But all that had changed in the blink of an eye—or maybe in a flash of lightning. He was in full caretaker mode now.

"I've got it," I said, wincing as I shifted to pull my phone out of my back pocket. I didn't like how damp the seat of my pants already felt. "I'll just make the call. I wouldn't say no if you wanted to pop the heating pad I have on the table beside my bed into the microwave, though. Three minutes."

"Sure," Jesse said, striding across the living room on his long legs and heading into my bedroom.

I got a full blast of his cedar scent as he walked past me. It was so powerful that a gush of slick leaked out of me like someone had turned on a faucet. I was mortified, especially since I felt it soak the back of my trousers, but there was no time to wallow in embarrassment. I would contemplate the implication of the fact that I'd never reacted so strongly to an alpha before in my life later.

"Phillip?" Dad answered after one ring. "Where are you, son? This storm came out of nowhere."

Somewhere near Dad, I heard Papa say, "It did not, Sal.

The forecast was spot on. If you would just watch the weather report in the morning—"

"You can scold me all you want later, Nick," Dad said, then went on with, "I take it you and Mr. Armstrong made it to your cabin?"

"We did," I said, trying not to moan, "but a tree was struck by lightning, and Jesse says it came down on the bridge, smashing the whole thing."

"*Jesse* said that?" Dad asked.

I wanted to give him a piece of my mind over the way he said Jesse's name, but there wasn't time. "Can you get some sort of replacement bridge in place, like, now?" I asked, whining in spite of myself.

Dad hummed, then said, "Let me guess. Your heat is starting. Even though you insisted it would be another week and you'd be fine teaching the class."

"Could we do this later, Dad?" I sighed heavily. "I need Ty up here, preferably an hour ago."

"I'll see what I can do," Dad said, "but honestly, it isn't safe for anyone to go outside with this storm still raging, and I doubt it's going to be easy to replace that bridge, even with something temporary, until tomorrow at the earliest."

I made a sound that was half frustration, half pain from the cramp that gripped me. They were coming faster and harder than they usually did, which worried me.

I was left panting a little when I told Dad, "I don't know what to do."

Of all things, Dad laughed. "Yes, you do, son. You're an ESA instructor. Is Armstrong still with you?"

That was all he needed to say, really. I already knew what solution he would suggest. It was the only solution available.

"He hasn't been trained," I said in a flat voice.

As I spoke, I realized Jesse had come out of the bedroom with the heating pad and taken it to the kitchen. I was looking right at him as I spoke, and he glanced from the running microwave to me with a look that said he'd heard everything I'd just said and knew the implication.

Dad laughed even harder. "Son, alphas have been taking omegas through heat without training for millennia. And you're B&M's best ESA instructor. Do what you do best and instruct. Consider this a hands-on crash-course for Armstrong."

"He's only auditing the class," I argued. "He's not training to be an ESA."

"Well, you could always ride out your heat while he sits by and watches," Dad suggested with too much humor in his voice. "He's not going anywhere. You've got plenty of toys in your closet to help with the heat."

I wanted to hiss a whole string of expletives at my dad, but I had more sense than that.

"We don't have any choice, do we." It wasn't a question.

Jesse had wandered to the edge of the kitchen and stood leaning in the doorway with his arms crossed and a grim expression on his face. He knew which way the wind was howling.

"Use this as a teaching moment," Dad said. "That's the best advice I can give you. I'm not at all worried about you, son. Mr. Armstrong has been vetted as thoroughly as every alpha actually training to be an ESA. I trust him with your heat. And I trust Ty to finish teaching your class."

Those words meant a lot to me. They gave me the confidence to do what I needed to do.

"Okay, Dad," I sighed, easing up a little as my cramp subsided. "I'll call you if anything changes or if we run into trouble."

"Sure you will," Dad said with an annoying amount of teasing.

"We'll see you after your heat, Philly," Papa said, his voice slightly quieter, like he was standing right next to Dad, both of their ears to the phone.

"Bye," I said, ending the call to spare myself further embarrassment from the two of them.

The microwave dinged at about the same time, and another, distant roll of thunder sounded.

"I will do whatever I can to help you," Jesse said, then turned to head into the kitchen to fetch the heating pad.

I groaned and writhed on the sofa, but not with pain. The whole situation was just too embarrassing for words. I was a reasonably important person. I had a crucial job in a deeply important institute. I was respected by alphas, omegas, and betas throughout Barrington and beyond. It wasn't fair that I'd been reduced to a roiling ball of hormones.

And it was just going to get worse. It wasn't a rumor or an exaggeration that omegas turned slutty when they were in the throes of a heat wave.

I took a deep breath as Jesse returned to the living room with the heating pad.

"You heard that conversation?" I asked, eyeing him gingerly.

"Yep," he said.

I paused, accepted the heating pad, and asked, "Have you ever been with an omega in heat?"

Jesse winced and rolled his shoulders. "No. I dated an omega right out of college. But his first heat during the time we were together came right when we first started dating, and he said it was too soon for us. We'd broken up before his next one, which shouldn't have surprised me, given his dismissal of me for that first heat. Other than that, I've only dated betas."

I sucked in a breath and nodded. "So you don't really know what to expect," I said, paused, then went on with, "You don't really know what's going to happen to me."

"I just sat through a day's worth of classes about omegas in heat with you," he said. "I think I can handle it."

I wasn't sure if his attitude was returning or if he was genuinely trying to reassure me. I had no choice but to give him the benefit of the doubt.

"Okay," I said, muscling myself to sit. I cringed as slick squished out of me as I did. I should have put a towel down on the sofa. "We're going to treat this like a practicum," I said.

"A practicum?" Jesse's brow shot up.

"Yep. I'm going to give you a crash course in all the policies and procedures a B&M ESA uses when meeting up with an omega in heat," I said.

Jesse eyed me suspiciously. "Is that entirely necessary? I'm still not becoming an ESA, no matter what's going on here."

"Oh, it's necessary, alright," I said, looking up at him. I didn't know if it was the heat hormones or if Jesse really was that big, but I felt dwarfed by him and fragile, and desperate to have him spread me wide and fuck me until I went blind. Yep, I definitely had a case of the heat-slutties. "It's necessary for me to preserve a shred of my dignity."

Before he could protest, I went on with, "Every B&M ESA is issued a heat care pack. It contains all the supplies you would need when going on a call. I have a couple spares in the closet over there." I nodded to the closet near my bedroom door. "Go grab one."

"Okay."

Jesse stepped swiftly away from me on his long legs, thighs as big and strong as— I needed to focus. He pulled open the closet door, searched for a second, then pulled out a good-sized purple backpack.

"Is this it?" he asked.

I nodded, overheated, overstimulated, and starting to cramp again. "Bring it over here and open it," I said, panting.

Jesse walked back to the sofa and sat on the opposite end

from where I was half-sitting, half-sprawled, fighting like crazy against the instinct to drag my pants down, flip to my hands and knees, and present my dripping ass to him.

Jesse took the contents of the backpack out and spread them on his end of the sofa. A look of amusement cut through his seriousness when he set a fat anal plug on the cushion beside a box of industrial strength condoms designed especially for alphas in rut, a large bottle of spermicide, a copy of the ESA training manual, a laminated procedure card, and a bunch of other stuff I would explain to him later.

Of course, it was the plug that caught his attention. With a grin, he held it up to me. "Would this help?"

"Not now." I shook my head, trying not to die of embarrassment as I explained, "It's for between heat waves, to keep your, er, um, seed inside me for as long as possible."

Jesse's mouth twitched, and his eyes flashed with amusement, like the lightning that had rolled away outside. "Does that actually help?" he asked, twisting the plug to look at it from all angles. "I mean, I've heard that alpha cum has magical properties, but...."

"It doesn't have magical properties," I sighed with irritation. "But it does contain hormones and chemicals that react with omega anatomy to have a soothing, calming effect." I owed it to Jesse to be a hundred percent honest, so I went on with, "And an aphrodisiac."

Jesse's brow went up again. "So those aren't just rumors. You really do crave it when you're in heat."

"Yes," I admitted, flaring hot. Which was also an indication another pre-heat wave cramp was about to hit me. At least I could pretend to be purely clinical as I explained it to him. "Omegas experience an overwhelming need for...*it* when they're at the height of a heat wave. In their womb, their mouth, on their skin, everywhere. It...it can get a little messy."

"I guess that's what these are for," Jesse said, grinning like a fool as he took a thick pack of wipes from the bottom of the backpack. He took a second pack out after that and laughed. "Shit, do we really need so many?"

I prayed that the lightning would come back and strike me dead. "If we run out, I have more in the bathroom."

"If we *run out*?" Jesse's eyes went wide.

"We were going to talk about what omegas actually experience in their heat waves tomorrow," I said, then was cut off as another cramp hit. I curled in on myself, slick gushing from me.

"But I get to learn first-hand right now," Jesse said, serious again. He shoved the contents of the backpack aide and scooted toward me. "Are you sure you're alright? Jake, the omega I dated before, didn't have cramps this strong that one time. Well, he could have after he went off with his friend."

"I've never had them this strong either," I admitted, panting and grimacing. "I don't know why—"

I gave up the explanation as pain wracked me. The only thing that could soothe me was only two feet away, creating a noticeable bulge in Jesse's jeans.

"Okay, I know enough about this from class today to know we need to relocate to the bedroom. Fast," Jesse said.

I shook my head. "This is a teaching moment. I need to teach."

Jesse looked like he wanted to protest, but he must have understood my dignity was at stake. "Tell me what to do."

I gulped a few times, clutching my middle, and nodded. "We hadn't gone over the initiation procedure in class yet, but there's a card to walk you through it." I nodded to the card on the sofa...next to the plug.

Jesse picked it up and scanned it with a frown. "Really? You really ask all these questions before you get to...it?"

"No, *you* ask the questions," I panted. "The alpha asks and says everything on that card so that both the alpha and the omega are crystal clear about expectations and about everything they're about to engage in. And for liability reasons. So go ahead."

"Alright," Jesse said, a little doubtfully. He scanned over the card again, then repeated the words Papa had come up with decades ago. "'Thank you for trusting me to take you through your heat. My name is Insert Name Here, and I am here to help you. I have been through extensive training to prepare for this call, so you can trust me to be aware of your needs, to care for you in your most vulnerable moments, and to maintain strict confidentiality before, during, and after your heat waves.'" He paused and glanced over to me. "Are you certain all of that is necessary?"

I would have been annoyed if I wasn't bristling with pain and getting hornier by the second. "It was market tested by a focus group of—nnngg." That was all the explanation I had time for.

"Okay, okay," Jesse said, holding out his free hand to me, looking a little alarmed. "We'll talk about how you came up with this later, maybe." He cleared his throat, then kept reading from the card. "Do you confirm that you requested an Emergency Support Alpha from Bangers & Mash?"

"Yes," I answered, as though I were a client and not a distressed member of the founding family.

Jesse nodded and kept reading from the card. "Do you consent to allowing me to take you through your heat?"

"Yes," I ground out, the cramp getting worse.

"Do you acknowledge and accept that this will mean having intense sexual relations, including penetration and ejaculation?" He stared at the card for a moment, as if wondering why the question was necessary.

"Yes," I said, planning to explain later.

"Do you acknowledge and accept that I will knot you as part of the natural part of intercourse?"

"Yes."

"Do you acknowledge and accept that I will be with you continuously for the duration of your heat, no matter how long it lasts?"

"Yes, yes." Maybe it wasn't such a good idea to have the consent part of the procedure last so long. I needed to be naked, and I needed Jesse to be naked with me. I needed his skin against mine, his dick inside me, and his cum filling me or I might just die.

"Do you acknowledge and accept that I will assume full responsibility for your physical and emotional wellbeing during the course of your heat, and that this could but might not be limited to anal, oral, and womb penetration, the exchange of bodily fluids, and extensive aftercare?"

"Yes, please. Please get on with it. I don't think I can hold out anymore," I moaned, clawing clumsily at the buttons of my shirt to get it off.

Jesse turned the card over, then looked at me warily, like he was beginning to be genuinely concerned for my health and safety. "It says there's a release form that you were supposed to sign and that I should check now to make certain you signed it."

"And if this was an actual ESA call, we would have taken care of that already," I panted. "Now, take off your clothes."

"There's another part that says we discuss which contraception options you prefer," Jesse said, setting the card down and tugging his shirt out of his jeans.

"Condoms, spermicide," I blurted, feeling as though the words had little meaning. "I'm on the pill anyhow, but no omega should ever take chances."

"Right," Jesse said, unbuttoning his shirt and peeling out of it. "Not that I'm criticizing your class or the program at all," he said, breathing deeply and heavily as I fumbled to remove my shirt, then to attempt to make my fingers work open the fly of my trousers, "but you should really talk about how ridiculously horny alphas get when they're this close to an omega in heat. I feel like I'm about to lose my mind."

I nodded and somehow growled, "Second day lecture."

"Yeah, but it's never been this strong before," Jesse nearly roared. "I want to fuck you so hard and so deep right now that you taste me, and I want it to be dirty."

I would have come up with something to say to that, I was sure. Something. The dirty talk was proof that Jesse was reacting strongly to me, which was a good sign for the experience we were about to have.

But Jesse unbuttoned his jeans and thrust his hips up as he yanked them down over his hips, and as soon as his long, thick, hard alpha cock jumped up and jutted toward me, I burst into needy tears and lost the ability to think.

Chapter Five

Jesse

I'd never seen anything like it before. In the course of a few minutes, Phillip went from the strong, admirable, slightly too serious teacher that I'd met that morning to a whimpering, weeping, writhing horn-ball.

And I liked it.

"Let's get you to the bedroom," I said, kicking my way out of my jeans and standing.

I scooped Phillip, half undressed, into my arms as if he were a baby. He'd managed to get his shirt halfway off, and since I was naked at that point, it meant lots of skin-on-skin contact. Phillip was as hot as a furnace, and all that touching made me want to forget the bedroom and drop him to the floor so I could fuck him right then and there.

"Condoms, condoms," Phillip gasped, one arm flailing toward the stuff from the ESA backpack scattered across the sofa.

"I'll come back for them," I said as I walked around the sofa, nearly running toward the bedroom.

"Don't forget," Phillip panted.

Part of me thought that was a ridiculous thing to say. A bigger part understood full well. I could hardly rub two brain cells together as I hurried into Phillip's bedroom and deposited him on the bed. I didn't have the presence of mind to notice anything about the room other than the queen-size bed.

It was like ripping off a patch of skin to leave Phillip there so that I could run back into the living room to get the box of condoms. My cock stood straight up, already leaking pre-cum, and my balls seemed to be expanding with seed instead of pulling up, like they usually did during sex. With a fleeting, humorous smirk, I told myself I was gearing up to shoot the mother of all loads.

I grabbed more than just the condoms from the sofa. I took a package of the wipes and the spermicide too. I probably should have shoved everything back into the backpack and taken it into the bedroom with me, but a groan from Phillip made me feel like there was a giant rubber band connecting us, and I had to race back into the bedroom with what I had.

I nearly dropped everything when I stepped back into the bedroom only to find Phillip on his hands and knees on the bed, his raised ass pointed toward me. His knees were spread far enough to leave him wide open, and his slightly dilated hole stood out against the pink flesh of his ass. Slick dripped from him like I'd never seen before, sliding down over his taint to spread across his balls. Maybe it was just my imagination, but it seemed to glisten like the juice of the most delicious fruit ever created.

"Fuck," I growled, marching to the bed and practically throwing everything I held onto the coverlet. "*Fuck*, that's the most beautiful thing I've ever seen."

"Fuck me, Jesse," Phillip panted, writhing so that his hips made small, circular motions, like I was already in him and he was milking my throbbing cock. "I need you inside me. Fuck me hard. I want all of you in me. Now. Now!"

I wanted that more than I wanted to breath. My dick twitched and dripped like it never had before. But instead of just walking right up to Phillip and shoving inside, I positioned myself behind him and brushed my hands over the round globes of that spectacular ass of his.

He felt amazing—hot and smooth and soft. I needed to touch him, needed to mark him as if my hands were brands and they would leave scars. I smoothed my way up over his back and sides, then down over his ass to his thighs.

"Oh, God!" Phillip moaned. "Yes! More! Touch me more. Spank me. Bruise me. Claim me and take me!"

I nearly came right then, but somehow managed to hold it in. I'd never really been one for kink in the bedroom, but the urge to do everything Phillip wanted me to do was overpowering.

"You want it rough, omega?" I growled, bending over him so that my much larger body encompassed his, speaking into his ear and fighting the urge to bite his lobe. My dick smacked against his crease as I did, getting coated with slick in the process, but I wasn't positioned right to penetrate him. I rubbed my throbbing cock over his dripping crease all the same. "You want this fat alpha dick in you?"

"Yes," Phillip whimpered. "God, yes!"

I reached around to stroke my hands over his chest, pinching his nipples and eliciting a wild cry from him. Phillip supported his weight and mine as I did, which was a testament to his deceptive strength. My urge to touch him everywhere was still there, and I moved from his nipples down over his stomach to grasp his straining cock.

He came immediately, which surprised both of us. We'd

talked in class that afternoon about how, during heat, omegas had a hair-trigger on their orgasms and how they generally experienced too many to count during each heat wave, but seeing it in action was something else. Small amounts of hot cum spilled over my fingers, but it was the twitching jerk of his cock and balls that told me the orgasm was intense for him.

And yet, it apparently wasn't even close to satisfying for him.

"I need it," Phillip groaned, pleasure-drunk and mindless. "Fuck me. Get in me. Fuck me and knot me. Now! Please! *Please!*"

I intended to do as he asked when I straightened, in position behind him, but his cum on my fingers was too inviting. I raised my hand to my mouth and sucked it off my fingers, like it was fresh honey. I'd never really been the sort to taste cum while having sex either, but now I couldn't get enough.

It made me want to taste other things from him. With a grunt, I shifted back and bent down so that I could kiss and lick the mounds of his ass, then practically buried my face against his dripping hole. I licked around the edges, nearly losing my mind with pleasure at the sweet taste of his slick. I suddenly couldn't get enough of it, like it was ambrosia and the cure for everything that had ever ailed me.

"Please, please!" Phillip moaned, writhing as I ate him out. I had the sense he was coming again, and hard.

His movements only pushed his hole closer to my mouth, so I did what came naturally and thrust my tongue into him. We both made ridiculous sounds of pleasure then. His dripping wet hole was the most inviting thing in the world, and I made sinful, slurping sounds as I thrust into his heat, his ring shivering around me, like it wanted to be stretched wider.

Omegas were the ones with a reputation for being slutty when in heat, but I felt like a depraved whore as I licked up his slick, loving the way it spread all over the bottom half of my face. I couldn't get enough of it, I needed to—

I felt an impending orgasm before I could finish the thought, and I wasn't going to be able to hold it back for long. I had to be inside Phillip, and I had to be there yesterday.

By some miracle, I remembered Phillip's request for a condom at the last second. I reached to the side and ripped into the box, tore through the wrapping, and got it on just in the nick of time. I could only pray that I got it on right, because I couldn't hold myself back for another second.

I grabbed Phillip's hips and slammed into him with way more force than I would ever have dreamed of using with a partner. I didn't even give him time to prepare or adjust. I would have been appalled with myself, but Phillip cried out with such ecstasy and jerked back against me, drawing me deeper.

"Yes! Yes!" he cried and shouted. "Fuck me hard! Yes! Harder! Deeper! Blow my mind out!"

He continued shouting nonsense with pleasure as I slammed into him over and over. It was the best thing I'd ever felt. I went fast and hard for a few thrusts, then pulled almost all the way out and fucked him with slow, long strokes, only to speed up again. It felt different than other guys I'd fucked. It was somehow tighter, hotter, and the angle felt different. It was so, so good, though.

I wasn't even sure when I started coming, just that my whole body felt it. I roared like an animal and slumped over Phillip, bracing my arms on either side of his body so I could use all my strength to pound him mercilessly. Phillip moaned and shouted and thrashed hungrily, and judging by the contractions I felt through my dick, he was coming hard and continuously as I brutalized him.

When my knot started to form, it came as such a shock that it took my breath away. Knotting was something teenage boys giggled about, breeding-age men bragged about, and old men reminisced about fondly. I'd never been with an omega during heat before, so I'd never experienced one. That was my very first, and it was every bit as mind-blowing as I'd ever been told.

It was one thing on paper. The muscle and tissue at the base of an alpha cock filled with blood and expanded while inserted in an omega breeding canal so that he was locked inside, unable to pull out. Very technical and biological.

It was another thing entirely in reality. My knot formed, Phillip cried out with pleasure, and probably a little pain, and bore down on me, and my over-filled balls felt like they exploded.

"Fuck, fuck!" I growled, hugging Phillip tight around his middle and jerking into him like the world was coming to an end.

I had little range of movement while locked inside him, but the urge to thrust and move had grown exponentially. My cock strained and jerked and felt like it was expanding too as I used Phillip hard. Even with his strength, he couldn't support us, and we collapsed flat on the bed. That seemed to sheath me tighter, and as I surged into him harder and harder, shooting more cum into him than I thought I had in me, I was afraid I might crush him.

But Phillip continued to moan and shudder, completely insensible. One of my hands was trapped against his stomach right above the tip of his cock, and I felt his cum gush over my fingers in hard, steady pulses. I wasn't certain if he was coming again or if he'd never stopped.

I couldn't stop, that much was certain. I was glad they made condoms specifically designed for the reservoir of cum spilling out of me. I kept rocking and pushing deeper and deeper into Phillip, until my sheathed cock rammed up against a barrier, then forced the tip right through. That set Phillip off into another round of spasms that had him weeping and shuddering with orgasm.

It did something to me too. I was already coming, but something about the way whatever gripped me massaged my tip had me soaring with ecstasy. I couldn't tell if I closed my eyes or if they rolled back into my head, and I wasn't sure if my orgasm grew stronger or if I started to have a seizure of some sort. All I knew was that it was the fucking best thing that had ever happened to me.

I didn't know how long it lasted, but when I could think and breathe again, I was still lodged deep within Phillip, still locked inside him by my knot. Phillip's body had gone still—so much so that I was worried I'd killed him for a moment.

"Phillip, are you okay?" I gasped, pulling back as much as I could while still knotted to him, bracing myself on my arms.

I nearly cried with relief when Phillip wriggled a bit and groaned. He wasn't dead.

"I'm...okay," he panted.

Relief washed through me, and I slumped over him again. A moment later, a sense of responsibility and the need to take charge filled me.

"Let's get us a little more comfortable," I said.

Phillip nodded weakly, then allowed me to manhandle him farther onto the bed and the right way around. It was strange and awkward to position the two of us in bed while locked together, but the sense of peace and wellbeing that radiated from Phillip, and that filled me, made the strangeness of it minor.

As soon as I had the two of us settled on our sides, my larger body spooning and sheltering Phillip's as we remained firmly joined, we both breathed a sigh of relief.

"This is my first knot ever," I said, then immediately felt self-conscious to admit to something so intimate.

Phillip twisted to look at me over his shoulder. "Really?"

He looked so sweet and innocent in my arms, even though everything that had just passed between us and the way we'd both turned into complete whores was anything but innocent.

I nodded, stroking his side, arm, and thigh absently. The first heat wave might have been over, but I still felt the visceral need to touch him all over, in every way. "It's my first omega heat, remember? Alphas don't knot unless they're with an omega in heat."

Phillip grinned saucily at me. "Now you sound like the teacher. That's my job."

I laughed. "That's actually my job too, remember? I teach at Olivarez High."

"Oh, yeah," Phillip said, his smile turning sweet and hazy. "We have a lot in common, then."

A pang of affection tugged at my heart. "Yeah, we do," I said, circling my arms around him and snuggling him close. I flexed my hips as I did, sinking deeper into him and causing us both to gasp. It wasn't the same as during the crest of the wave, though. "Do you teach more than just these training classes?" I asked.

It was a bizarre time for a getting to know you conversation, but from what I understood, knots could last for half an hour, and until mine went down so I could separate, we were fused. Might as well get to know the man who'd just blown my mind a little better.

Phillip shook his head, then shrugged his shoulders in a movement that went through his whole body, bringing us closer together. "I thought about going into teaching, but it's hard for omegas to get teaching jobs, even with all the reforms. I teach at least one class a month, and sometimes I do remote, private coaching for alphas who live farther out from Barrington. The rest of the time, I do paperwork and program development."

The earlier part of his statement hit me hard, causing me

to tense. "Private coaching?" I asked. "Does that include having your heat serviced by your student?"

Phillip was silent for longer than I was comfortable with—not that I had any right to get all possessive over him. We'd only just met, after all.

And yet, it was like I'd known him my whole life.

"Sometimes," he admitted. "But only when there has been a prior arrangement to do so. Omegas go into heat two or three times a year, depending on age and genetics. Less often if they've just given birth. Some omegas take a full year or more to have another heat wave after giving birth. And conservatives can get as moralistic as they'd like, but it is infinitely easier on an omega's body and mind if they have an actual, living, breathing alpha take them through heat instead of using toys. Or betas, for that matter."

"Is it true omegas can die if they don't have an alpha for several heats in a row?" I asked about the rumor I'd heard.

Phillip nodded. "I don't know if there's any documentation of it, but I certainly feel that way." He paused, peeking up at me, looking a bit guilty. "Remember what I said about alpha cum having necessary hormones and chemicals in it?"

"Yeah?" I arched one eyebrow.

Phillip sighed. "I will admit, as good as that was—and I can honestly say that might be the best sex I've ever had—it wasn't enough. Condoms are necessary for contraception, and some of the hormones do make it past the latex barrier, but I don't feel satisfied, because I'm not swimming in your juices now."

I laughed. "Please don't ever use the phrase 'swimming in your juices' ever again."

He laughed with me. It felt so good, almost as good as the sex. "How about 'doused with your love potion'?"

I laughed harder. "Definitely not."

"Painted with your passion sauce?"

Now he was just being silly. And I loved it. I held him closer, kissing his neck and jaw as we both laughed. I pushed deeper into him as well, but already I felt my knot beginning to loosen. I was surprised that I didn't want it to go down. I wanted to feel him this close to me for a while longer. It was as if we hadn't just known each other for years, it was like we'd been together for years as well. All those feelings swelled in my chest.

"But seriously," Phillip went on, "it actually is important for me to have contact with your semen."

I arched an eyebrow. "How romantic."

Phillip chuckled, but I could tell he was exhausted. "Would you mind if I sucked you off during my next heat wave?" he asked, then yawned.

I propped myself on one arm so I could look down at him. "Did you actually just ask if you could blow me?"

The sheepish look he sent me was a direct contrast to his stern, teacher face, and it shot straight to my heart. "Yes?" he said, his face flushing.

"Sweetheart," I said with a smirk, "you never have to ask whether you can give me a blow job."

He chuckled, but I could tell he was about to fall asleep. "I might end up latching on like a barnacle and sucking you dry."

I growled with lust and settled against his back again, moving in him and sending ripples of stimulation all through my groin and into my belly. "Any time, sweetheart. Any time."

He mumbled something in reply, but the words were lost as sleep took him. Come to think of it, he had mentioned something about omegas needing to sleep between heat waves.

He'd also mentioned that the waves increased in intensity through the first day, peaked on the second, and tapered off on the third. Which meant we had a hell of a lot more to look forward to.

Chapter Six

Phillip

It had been good. It had been so, so good. At twenty-four, it was far from my first heat, and I'd had an alpha take me through for all but one of those—one of the perks of my dads owning and operating an ESA service. But it had never felt as good as it had with Jesse, even though he'd been wearing a condom.

I wanted to chalk it up to coincidence, but the quiet nagging in the back of my head wouldn't let me. There could be a reason why heat sex with Jesse had blown my mind and left me feeling like a quivering puddle of lust. There could be a reason his scent was so overpowering to me, and why I kept thinking I heard him say something. But it was almost unheard of. We'd just met, after all. It usually took years before a relationship hit that point.

Unless....

The room was dark, Jesse's knot had gone down, and he'd

pulled out and cleaned up by the time I woke from my heat-exhaustion nap. Jesse still spooned me, and the way our bodies touched in so many ways felt fantastic. As soon as sleep fully left me, I groaned and stretched in Jesse's embrace, then twisted so that I faced him.

Jesse had been asleep as well, but he woke when I turned. A lazy smile spread across his face even before he opened his eyes as I wrapped myself around his large solid body. God, it felt good! I was already hard again, and I could feel another heat wave building in my core.

"I'd say good morning, but I don't think it's anywhere close to morning yet," Jesse said in his deep bass voice.

I lifted myself up to look past Jesse at the clock on the bedside table. "It's not even midnight," I said.

Which probably meant not everyone on the rest of the mountain had gone to sleep yet.

"I have to call my dads to let them know I'm alright," I said, flinching as though I would sit and roll out of bed, but really not wanting to.

My body felt rubbery and used, and a little bit sore. There was an obvious reason for that, of course. I closed my eyes and let out a breath as I remembered how good the first heat wave had been. It didn't matter how many times I taught about how amazing it felt to have a dick pounding away in an omega's breeding passage, actually experiencing it was out of this world. No wonder some omegas took drugs or resorted to dangerous toys to open that passage when they weren't in heat just to feel it.

"Do you want me to go grab your phone from the living room?" Jesse asked with a laugh.

I opened my eyes to find him grinning down at me. Fuck, he was gorgeous. That wasn't just the hormones and heat haze talking either. Jesse Armstrong was objectively handsome. His blue eyes sparkled, and his chiseled face screamed alpha virility.

Well, I knew first-hand how virile he was now. And it would be even better without a condom.

That thought had me sucking in a breath as I remembered another detail from our mating. He'd breeched my womb. On the very first try, during the very first heat wave, the head of his cock had penetrated the ring of muscle guarding my womb. Holy fuck. In all of my previous heats, that had only happened to me one time, and only then during the strongest heat wave. I'd been with a trusted friend for that heat three years ago.

Omega wombs only opened up like that when the alpha involved was deeply, deeply compatible with the omega. Rumor was that a full-body orgasm—like the one I'd had that made me delirious with pleasure—only happened if the alpha and omega were a bonded pair.

But instant pair-bonding was considered a bit of a fairy tale these days. Dad and Papa were pair-bonded, but they'd been together for thirty-five years.

I'd met Jesse less than twenty-four hours before. It was impossible that we'd pair-bonded after one heat wave...with a condom.

"I'll get your phone," Jesse said, laughing even harder, as he pulled away from me and climbed out of bed. "You're still too heat-drunk to think straight."

Maybe that was it. Maybe that was why I whimpered and felt like someone had ripped my skin off when Jesse moved away from me. The anxiety I felt when he left the room, even though I could still hear him in the living room, was horrifying. It was as bad as the pleasure between us had been good.

Which was rumored to be another sign of pair-bonding. Bonding caused all sorts of craziness during heat, for both the omega and the alpha.

But it didn't happen at first sight. That was a myth.

Jesse ran back into the room in less than a minute carrying not only my phone, but the wipes and plug from the ESA kit.

"Oh, thank God!" He breathed heavily, as though the place were on fire. "I don't know why, but I could have sworn you were in trouble the second I stepped out of the room. Like I could hear you screaming in my head or something."

I slumped back against the pillow, dread and joy and astonishment forming in my gut. Dad had described that feeling about Papa when they'd been in the middle of a heat.

I was going to say something by way of explanation to Jesse, but the way his eyes dragged over my exposed, flushed, aroused body as I sprawled across the bed told me the explanation would have to wait for another day.

"Fuck, Phillip," he growled, coming to the bed and throwing the wipes and plug in the corner, then handing me my phone. "You'd better make that call quick. I feel like I'm about to explode just looking at you all sweet and vulnerable like this."

In fact, as soon as he'd dropped the wipes and plug, he'd started stroking himself, seemingly without being aware of it. His muscled, alpha body looked so strong and overpowering as he knelt between my legs, stroking his massive dripping cock, that my hands began to shake. All alphas were well-endowed, but how had I not realized that Jesse was gargantuan. That could have been the heat hormones too, though.

I fumbled with my phone, tapping it to life and calling Dad with shaking hands. All the while, my gaze stayed locked on Jesse's body, on his broad shoulders and chest and thick arms, the hair dusting his chest and making a line to his groin, his thick thighs, and his surprisingly graceful hands as they caressed his swollen cock. His cockhead already dripped with pre-cum, and every stroke seemed to push more out.

"Phillip. How are you doing?" Dad's voice asked sleepily as the call connected.

"Fine," I lied in a hoarse voice. "Heat. Y'know."

I had no idea how I was going to form the words to have

this conversation with a rampant Jesse towering over me, lust glazing his eyes, sex oozing from him.

"Is Jesse doing a good job of taking you through?" Dad asked. Or at least I thought he did. My thoughts were mush already.

"Yeah," I gasped. "Howizza...." I had no idea what I was trying to say or ask.

Dad chuckled. I heard Papa ask something near him. Dad answered, but I wasn't really paying attention. Jesse's breath was coming in shallow pants now, and sweat had broken out on his torso. He was practically shaking with the effort not to dive on me.

"Sounds like you're about to hit another wave," Dad said. "So I'm going to assume I know why you're calling. We did walk up and take a look at the bridge after the storm passed. It's toast, but we should be able to come up with something temporary tomorrow to make do until a new bridge can be constructed. But something tells me you won't need to worry about that for a couple days.

"Ty is happy to take over the rest of your class," Dad went on, though I barely heard him. "So as long as you have enough food and water up there, everything is good. You and Mr. Armstrong enjoy yourselves."

I grunted and ended the call. I couldn't remember why I'd called anyhow. I had wanted to ask Dad something?

It didn't matter. It wasn't important. I tossed my phone aside, aiming for the bedside table, but missing. The phone fell to the floor with a clatter. I didn't care, I only wanted one thing.

"Give me that cock," I gasped, struggling to sit.

I didn't make it all the way to a sitting position before Jesse caught me behind the neck with his free hand and hefted me up until I was half sitting, half leaning against the pillows and the headboard. He didn't hesitate at all before bringing his dick to my mouth.

Before I could open my mouth, he dragged his cockhead across my lips, smearing them with pre-cum like it was lip gloss. I breathed in sharply, the scent of cedar and sex and my own sweet scent—which I only noticed when I was in heat and it was overpowering—filled my nose. I licked my lips, tasting Jesse's pre-cum, then brazenly dragged my tongue across the head of his cock.

Jesse made a sound of pleasure like nothing I'd ever heard, and right away, hot jets of cum spilled across my tongue and lips and chin. I groaned with pleasure, my own cock throbbing with a dry orgasm, and lapped up every drop. I licked and circled his entire, huge mushroom head as I did, causing him to gasp and growl and come even more. Then I closed my mouth around just his head and sucked and teased it like my life depended on it.

"Shit, Phillip, that feels incredible!" Jesse boomed.

I bore down on him, nudging him to shove into my throat. Words like, "Fuck my face, make me choke, own my throat until I can't breathe," rang in my head, but they were impossible to say aloud with a mouth full of dick.

Jesse seemed to hear them anyhow. He braced his hands on the wall behind the headboard and jerked his hips into my mouth, going deeper with each thrust. I'd never been such a cockslut before, and even though I started to retch as another burst of orgasm had Jesse spilling cum down my throat, I wouldn't have had it any other way just then.

I grabbed his ass as the muscles there clenched and flexed with his thrusts, digging my fingertips in hard. Jesse let out a howl, and just as his orgasm started to subside, it started up again. I couldn't swallow fast enough, and cum and spit spilled from my mouth, dribbling down my chin to my chest.

But true to what I'd told him earlier, the effect was as if someone had poured liquid pleasure on me.

Jesse either remembered those words or he sensed that I was in real danger of choking. He pulled out of my gaping, panting mouth and finished off his orgasm by pumping cum all over my chest and stomach. I knew logically from teaching it a dozen times that alphas with an omega in heat produced epic levels of cum, but even I was astounded at how it kept coming and coming until I was soaked with it.

Jesse finally sank onto his haunches when the spurts stopped and just gaped at me and at what he'd done, desperately trying to catch his breath as he did. "Two packs of wipes are not enough," he gasped, wiping his mouth with the back of his hand as if he were the one with a face full of cum.

I laughed. I couldn't help it. Now that I was saturated with his seed, inside and out, I felt euphoric. Everything was wonderful and happy. I felt amazing, ecstatic.

Well, almost everything was wonderful and happy.

My ass cramped, and I became aware of the fact that I was sitting in a puddle of slick. At some point in the face fucking, I'd come as well. Jesse's wasn't the only cum decorating me. My cock was still hard, though, and everything on the inside screamed out for a share of the bounty.

I winced and groaned and writhed with the cramps, then somehow managed to say, "Fuck me, Jesse. I need you inside me. I need a fuckload of cum inside me right now."

Jesse let out a tired, wry laugh and reached for the box of condoms. "Reason and logic say I shouldn't have it in me for another couple of years after that fountain of cum, but my balls feel like they're working overtime right now."

"No condom!" I gasped as if he'd reached for a weapon. "I need you raw. I need that cum all over my insides."

Jesse paused and drew back from reaching for the box. He looked at me with a strange look—one that I wanted to slap off his face while ordering him to fuck me senseless. "That protocol sheet says I'm supposed to take every precaution possible not to get you pregnant."

"Spermicide," I gasped, gesturing wildly toward the bottle that we somehow hadn't manage to kick off the side of the bed yet. "That's why it's in the kit. Use it like lube. And I'm on the pill, so it won't matter."

"Is that part of the official ESA heat support protocol, Mr. Mash?" Jesse asked, a light of teasing in his eyes as he reached for the bottle of spermicide.

"Fuck you," I gasped in return. "No." I shook my head and hooked my hands under my knees, pulling my legs up and apart to stretch my drenched hole wide. "Fuck me. Fuck me hard with that huge alpha cock of yours. Fuck me all the way up to my womb and make me scream!"

That got Jesse's attention and put the fear of God in him. He popped open the cap of the spermicide bottle and poured it over the head of his cock—which was once again hard and huge and dripping. My whole body started to shake at the sight of it.

Jesse inched closer, coating the fingers of his right hand with spermicide as he went. He then inserted those fingers and the spermicide into my hungry hole, finger-fucking me in the most utilitarian way possible.

Utilitarian or not, I was already so sensitive that I started coming as soon as he curled his fingers up to hit my prostate. I moaned and bucked like my life depended on it as my dick throbbed and twitched with a mostly dry orgasm. A few drops made it out, but unlike an alpha's, my omega body's resources were occupied with other things besides making semen at that moment. Relatively little semen was produced by omegas in heat, even though their orgasms were frequent and long-lasting.

Jesse threw the bottle of spermicide aside and pushed

himself hard into me, as though he couldn't help it. I'm not sure he could have stopped himself if he'd tried. Between my slick and the spermicide, I was so wet that he made squelching sounds as he pounded into me, reaching deeper with each thrust.

I would have laughed at that, but the friction of his thick cock against the lit-up nerves and glands of my breeding passage had me howling with pleasure. It really was that good to have an alpha cock rubbing that secret part of me. Alphas and betas could never understand the brain-melting pleasure that part of an omega's anatomy gave us. Logically, I understood it was nature's way of motivating omegas to breed. In practice, it was like every cell in my body was only sleeping in my ordinary life, but they all came online at once as Jesse fucked the daylights out of me.

"Harder! Harder!" I screamed. "I want all of you! Knot me and fuck me hard!"

Whether it was coincidence or Jesse was just very good at following orders, he did just that. The breath rushed out of my lungs as his knot formed just inside the overstretched ring of muscle at my entrance. Within seconds, he was locked inside of me, stretching me to my limits. It was painful for the first minute or so, but that pain had an otherworldly feeling, especially when Jesse kept thrusting, pushing deeper and deeper with loud grunts, sweat dripping from his massive body, until he bumped up against the entrance to my womb again.

And just like before, even though it was unheard of, my womb responded to him by opening like a flower and letting his tip in.

That was when he started to come. I knew it because I could feel it, whether I was supposed to or not. I felt the relentless gush and spurt of his seed filling me as deeply as it was possible to be filled. I felt his warmth and his essence fuse itself with my soul. I felt the beating of his heart in time with mine, as though we were one being who had spent too long apart but was joined together at last.

And then I felt nothing but heat and sunlight and joy as an orgasm like nothing I'd ever experienced before swallowed me. Every bit of me was soaked in pleasure. It raced through me like blood and fire, electricity and oxygen. I wasn't sure I even had a body anymore, or if I did, I left it behind as my soul tangled up with his. I could still feel the pull and pressure of his thrusts, but it was like I was inside out and made of light and pleasure. I wrapped myself around him and through him, like I could hear every one of his thoughts and like I knew him inside and out.

I don't know how long it took me to come down from that place, but I was still catching my breath, and so was Jesse, when reality settled back in on me. Jesse was still knotted firmly within me, but he'd stopped moving and was just trying to catch his breath too. We were both drenched in sweat and slick and cum, and not only would the sheets need to be washed, but I might have to get a new mattress once my heat was over as well.

"That was...." Jesse started to speak, but couldn't find the words.

"Yeah," I gasped in return.

Our eyes met, and it was like the world held still for a moment.

Then he surged into me and kissed me.

It was our first kiss. As hot as the first two heat waves had been, we hadn't kissed. I didn't usually kiss at all when I was in heat. Ironically, it felt too intimate. But as Jesse slanted his mouth over mine and drew my tongue into his mouth with surprising tenderness, all I wanted to do was kiss him back.

I looped my arms loosely around his shoulders, only vaguely aware that I was still on my back and my legs circled his waist—though I could already feel them slipping as all energy left me. Jesse balanced himself so tenderly above me, moaning as he fused our mouths together, kissing me with gentleness that was a stark contrast to the brutality of the way he'd fucked me.

"I love you," he whispered between kisses, peppering them all over my face and neck before coming back to kiss my mouth with lingering passion again.

"I love you, too," I said against his mouth.

Even though I knew it was the heat hormones, even though I was well-versed on the false sense of closeness and affection that developed between an alpha and omega in heat, even though my brain told me they were just words whispered in the heat of passion and I didn't know the man who held me and kissed me as I fell asleep in spite of myself, I believed it. I believed I loved Jesse Armstrong, and that our souls were now inextricably linked, even though it was impossible.

Chapter Seven

Jesse

Nothing could have prepared me for taking an omega through heat. It was hands down the hottest sex I'd ever had, so I understood why some alphas would have wanted to be an ESA. But after the third heat wave in the middle of the night, I didn't know how any alpha could view the whole thing as an emotionless job that needed to be done and then left behind.

It wasn't just the knotting that made it hot either. It was the whole thing, the way I just had to touch Phillip everywhere, the way he was hungry for my cock and cum, the way every nerve ending in my body fired at once as I slid into Phillip's amazing wetness, and the way both of our orgasms lasted ten times longer than I had thought was humanly possible.

Or maybe it was just Phillip.

There was something deeply special about Phillip Mash. I'd blurted out that I loved him after that second heat wave, and even though I didn't repeat the words during or after the third, I didn't feel like I wanted to take them back. And when I woke late into the morning after that third wave, even though I wasn't knotted in him anymore, I just wanted to hold Phillip close to me and breathe in his essence.

The storm that had wreaked havoc the night before had completely passed at some point during the night, and bright, glittering sunlight pored through Phillip's bedroom window as I came to full wakefulness. We hadn't shut the curtains the night before. We'd been just a wee bit preoccupied. Then again, Phillip's cabin was so remote that there was no one around to peer through the windows and see our sticky, disheveled, still a bit overheated bodies twined together on the bed—which looked like it had been the scene of a particularly raunchy Jell-O wrestling match.

That made me laugh, even though part of me felt completely disgusting.

"What are you laughing at?" Phillip said groggily. We'd slept with me spooning him from behind, so he twisted to glance over his shoulder at me.

The sight of him all sleepy and heat-wrecked was so beautiful that I caught my breath. Objectively, he was a mess. We'd run out of wipes after that third heat, and he had spots of dried cum all over his chest and shoulders, and mats of it in his hair. His skin was still flushed pink, telling me we weren't even halfway through and there would be more fucking mayhem in as little as a few minutes. His lips were swollen from all the kissing we'd done in that third wave, and I had a feeling that his hole was red and puffy and sore from the way I'd pounded him so hard and knotted him. But he was luminescent, and I loved him.

Loved *it*, I corrected myself. I loved it. I loved the way he looked, the feelings he gave me, and yes, I fucking loved the sex. But it was foolish to think I loved *him*. We didn't know each other, not really.

"How do the trained ESAs stop themselves from feeling like they're head over heels in love with their clients?" I blurted out the question, then immediately felt stupid.

Phillip flushed a darker, sexier shade of red, then muscled himself around to face me. He winced as he did, telling me his omega body had taken a beating, and would continue to take one for another couple of days.

"They don't, usually," he said with a sober look of honesty in his eyes. He rested his palm against the matted chest hair over my heart. My heart immediately began to beat in time with the pulse I could swear I felt in his hand. He stared at his hand for a while before looking up into my eyes. "ESAs are perfectly capable of taking an omega through their heat with complete detachment. I mean, it's not like they're cold or anything," he quickly corrected himself. "We only hire alphas who have a compassionate streak and who are genuinely decent human beings. That's why the application process is so stringent."

I had a feeling I knew what he was getting at with that comment, even though it was a diversion. That was the weird thing. I was absolutely certain I knew what Phillip really meant, no matter what he said. Like I had some sort of sixth sense of him after all we'd done.

"So an alpha doesn't usually feel like he's known the omega he's with for his entire life, even though they've just met?" I asked, placing my hand over his.

We stared at each other for a long time in silence. The answer to my question was right there in Phillip's eyes. Something unique had happened between us, something special. Something that I had a feeling didn't happen every day.

I tried to recall everything I knew about alpha/omega pairings, the deep ones. I went through a list of older alpha/omega couples I knew, men who had been together their whole lives, for decades. And I knew one male alpha and female omega couple too. They were the happiest people I'd ever come across in my life. It felt trite and cheesy to say, but they were like two halves of the same whole.

I'd never once stopped to ask any of them how that had happened or how long it took to feel that way.

"We'd better get up and eat something and take a shower before my next heat wave," Phillip said, breaking the moment between us. "We should start to see more time between waves, now that we're into the second day, but they'll be even more intense today."

"Is that how things normally happen?" I asked as we broke apart and climbed off opposite sides of the bed.

The bed really did look like a complete disaster. Not only were the sheets rumpled and pulled off the mattress, used wipes were discarded wherever I'd thrown them, the half-empty bottle of spermicide sat in one corner of the bed, the discarded box of condoms had scattered all over the foot, and the one used condom we'd tried hung off the foot of the bed, looking engorged and completely gross.

I stared at the bed like it was a gruesome crime scene as Phillip said, "It is. The first day of an omega heat is intense, with heat waves coming right on top of each other. By the second, things have evened out a bit," he said as he walked to the en suite bathroom, gesturing for me to follow him. "Well, they even out if an omega has been with an alpha. If the omega is trying to go it alone, it's like being repeatedly slammed by a cricket bat without pause for days. Alphas make all that better. Magic cum, remember?"

He sent me a saucy look over his shoulder as he went straight to the shower and turned it on. That look—which was so different from the stoic, serious teacher I'd met in the classroom the day before—combined with his filthy appearance, went straight to my heart, which seemed to beat a steady rhythm of "Love him. Love him. Love him."

"So, I take it the hormones and chemicals I just spewed all over you and filled you with appease whatever horny heat gods live inside of you," I said, making light of the moment as the shower heated.

Phillip laughed. "Yeah, something like that. But those heat gods are greedy, and they'll want more." He laughed again as he tested the shower temperature, then said, "I'll have to start using that analogy in my classes. Come on."

I blinked as he stepped into the spray. "You want me to shower with you?"

"Yes," he said with a broad smile, practically tugging me into the shower with him. "For one, I don't know how much time we have before the next wave. I can already feel it building, so we should economize our time to get as much done as possible."

"We still have to eat too," I said.

"Right." He wasted no time grabbing the soap and rubbing it all over my torso. "And for another," he said, slightly more breathless, "I don't think I could handle being more than a few feet apart from you at the moment."

He tilted his head down, as if he were concentrating on his task, but there was a sheepish look in his eyes that I found completely endearing.

"Is that normal?" I asked, taking a bottle of shampoo from the shelf behind him and squeezing some into my hand.

I started washing his hair as he scrubbed my body and answered, "It's ordinary for an omega to be clingy throughout their heat. Biologically, it's in the omega's best interest to stay as close to the alpha who could protect them when they're in such a weakened state." He glanced up at me as I used the shampoo still on my hands to clean the back of his neck. "I'll be weak as a baby by the end of the day, after a few more heat waves. I might not be able to stand or take care of my own needs."

"So you said in class yesterday," I said with a nod. I smiled. "Don't worry, sweetheart, I'll take care of you."

I wasn't sure what gave those words so much emotion, but I had to kiss Phillip's lips lightly after saying them.

Phillip's eyes lit up like the morning sky, then he blushed beautifully and went back to scrubbing me.

We concentrated on washing each other, which proved to be one of those things, like kissing, that was ten times more intimate than all the hard fucking we'd done. We got in a fair number of giggles as well as we shamelessly washed each other's most intimate places. Phillip was wet again—or maybe still wet was a better way to put it—and all the washing and rinsing in the world couldn't have stopped him from leaking.

"Omega biology is so embarrassing during heat," he lamented as I toweled him dry after the shower, soaking the towel with more than just water.

"I dunno," I said with a casual shrug. "I think it's super hot."

I was on my knees behind him, and I couldn't resist laying a quick kiss on one of his ass cheeks.

That kiss sent a quiver through his body that I could feel, and whether deliberately or on instinct, Phillip moved his feet farther apart and arched his back to stick his ass out.

I couldn't say no to his fresh, sweet-smelling ass in my face, so I dropped the towel and spread his cheeks wide, then kissed my way from the base of his spine, into his crease, and down to tongue his now dripping hole. I lapped it up, rubbing my tongue against his hole and around his rim, then thrusting it inside to slurp more of him.

Phillip leaned forward and braced himself against the bathroom wall, moaning with pleasure as he did. "That feels so good," he panted. "And the next wave hasn't even started yet."

"It hasn't?" I asked, rocking back. When he shook his head, I laughed. "You're just a slick fountain for me, in or out of a heat wave, right?"

I meant it as a joke, but the way he blushed and hid his face against his arm told me it wasn't a joke at all. It was better than that.

Something unusual was definitely going on.

I stood and leaned against the wall so that my much larger body encompassed his, bracing my hands on the walls beside his. "As much as I would love to bury my cock in that wet ass of yours and try to jumpstart the next wave, we really do need to eat something."

"You're right," Phillip gasped, arching his back into me so that our bodies made contact everywhere. "But for the record, I want your cock badly."

I sucked in a breath, my face buried in the side of his neck, and smiled. "This isn't normal, is it?" I asked.

Phillip pushed back against me slightly, and I took that as a sign to move so that he could turn around. To my surprise, he wore a serious face when he did.

"No, it's not," he said, placing a hand on my chest. He looked up at me with wisdom in his eyes. If I wasn't already hard, his touch and that look would have sent me there. "I have something I have to tell you," he went on. "But we really need to eat, because we don't have much time."

I knew what he meant, and I moved back to let him precede me out of the bathroom.

Neither of us dressed as we walked to the living room and on to the kitchen. From what Phillip had said in class the day before, omegas couldn't tolerate anything against their skin but their alpha when they were in the middle of heat. I didn't have any excuse to stay naked, but my cock was so hard that it would have been a nuisance to cover it.

"There should be protein shakes in your ESA kit," Phillip said, gesturing vaguely toward the empty backpack on the sofa. "The packs I have on hand haven't had the shakes added yet because they're perishable. The shakes are specially formulated to replenish a lot of the nutrients we've lost as quickly as possible. There isn't usually enough time for a five-course meal between heat waves."

"Yeah, tell me about it," I said with a smirk as Phillip pulled open his fridge door.

"Fuck, that feels good," he sighed as the cold air hit him.

I thought he might stay there forever, the way he closed his eyes and groaned, so I walked up behind him and reached in to take out two shakes—one with an orange, alpha label and the other with a purple, omega label. I figured they were each formulated differently, and that Phillip had both in his fridge because he'd known his heat was coming.

"We should probably change the sheets on the bed while we're able," I said, opening Phillip's shake and handing it to him, then pulling him away from the fridge.

He seemed to come out of a stupor slowly, blinking at his shake, as though he didn't know how he ended up with it. "You're right," he said.

We headed back to the bedroom, making a brief stop at a hall closet to gather clean sheets. It was quick work to strip the bed, since it was a mess already, and it took us slightly longer to put two bottom sheets on after.

"How long have you been a high school teacher?" Phillip asked as we worked, pausing to drink his shake as we did.

He was beating around the bush of whatever it was he wanted to tell me, I could feel it, but I would play along.

"Just two years," I said. "I went through college, then pursued a master's degree in Special Education, because I thought it would make me more hirable at the schools where I wanted to teach."

"Did it?" Phillip asked.

"Yeah, actually, it did," I said with a smile. "Olivarez High is one of the top high schools in Barrington, especially when it comes to omega education."

"And that's important to you?" Phillip looked at me with a particularly piercing stare.

"Very," I answered honestly. "One of the things that struck me in undergrad was all of the educational inequality omegas have experienced up until the last two decades or so. I wanted to work toward breaking through a lot of those stigmas and enabling omegas to live their best lives. I guess I have ambitions of being a guidance counselor on top of regular teaching."

Phillip's smile turned dreamy as we finished with the fitted sheets. "That's actually what I've been doing here. Helping omegas to live their best lives."

"And that means not being tied down in a marriage of necessity, or bearing child after child, right?" I asked, even though I knew it was true.

"Exactly," Phillip said.

"And I want to give them the tools and inspiration they need to have a career in whatever field they want, not just the ones their grandparents think are suitable," I said, reaching for my shake to drink the last of it. I could have used another, but I didn't want to go back to the kitchen to get it.

"It's funny how we both have the same sort of mission in life," Phillip said as he reached for his shake as well. "We're just working on it from different angles."

"Yeah, we are," I said, feeling as though those words were more significant than they seemed. Something occurred to me, and I blinked. "I think I suddenly understand why my principal, Mr. White, sent me up here for training, even though I'm not going to be an ESA."

"Oh?" Phillip walked around the bed to stand near me.

I could feel his next wave coming on and figured we should get to the point of the conversation fast.

"I think he wanted me to see what kind of choices my students could make once they reach heat age and need to worry about things like this," I said. "I think he wanted me to develop the empathy that comes with knowing what those students are going to go through so that I can advise them about how to integrate heat into the rest of their lives. At the very least, they need to know what their legal rights are in terms of time off of work for heat, no matter what profession they choose."

"Do you feel like you'll be able to have those sorts of discussions with them?" Phillip asked, moving even closer to me.

I laughed ironically. "It's never easy to talk to impressionable young people about sensitive topics like this, but this whole experience has opened my eyes to a lot of things I think I'm going to find very useful."

Phillip finished his shake and set the can down. He bent over more than he needed to as he set it on the bedside table, which was a flashing neon sign to show me he wanted to be bred hard again.

I almost laughed. Omegas really were slutty when they were in heat. Or, at least, Phillip was when he was in heat around me. But to be fair, I felt like an absolute whore myself. I couldn't think of anything but parting those silky ass cheeks and ramming into him.

"You'd better spill whatever it is you've been avoiding telling me for the last fifteen minutes," I said, my voice going rough and gravelly again, "because I can smell your next heat wave starting, and if I don't get my dick in that ass or down your throat soon, I might go out of my mind."

Phillip laughed and stepped over to me, draping his arms over my shoulders and plastering his body against mine.

I took that as an invitation to sweep him off his feet and to lay him flat on his back on the bed. He groaned and writhed at the way I covered him and jerked his already hard prick against mine, gasping at the pleasure that must have caused him.

"Phillip?" I scolded him, one eyebrow raised. "Spill it."

Phillip sighed and went deliciously pliant in my arms. But his expression turned serious as he looked up into my eyes.

"There's something I don't actually bring up in my class, because there isn't any scientific proof it exists," he said.

"What is that, sweetheart?" I asked, bending down to kiss his forehead, his nose, and his lips.

"It's um...." I muscled myself above him when he paused. His face was bright red, and not just from the heat wave. "I don't generally talk about bonding or fated mates," he said in a rush.

My heart clenched in my chest. Everyone had heard the fairy tales of fated mates. And bonding was a real thing. All of those couples who had been together for most of their lives that I knew were open about having bonded. It was something that developed over years though. Wasn't it?

I knew it wasn't. I knew immediately that was what had happened with me and Phillip. I knew it, and it changed my world right there, in that instant.

"We bonded," I said, blinking and muscling myself above him. "How did that happen?"

Phillip didn't even try to argue with me, which was all the confirmation I needed. "I don't know," he said. "But the more I talk to you, the more I see how much we have in common. Not just our professions and our missions in life, but I think probably our outlooks too."

"And that's it?" I asked. "That's all it takes to find your soulmate?" I grinned with joy, and a little silliness. "Fuck, that was easy."

Phillip laughed as well. "I don't know what happened," he said, sliding his hands over my chest. "It has to be a one-in-a-million thing. We just won the lottery."

"I like it," I said, lowering myself so I could kiss him again.

Phillip ate up my kiss like it was the first and last one he would ever get. He moved his arms to embrace me and wriggled his body suggestively under me.

I was certain the next words out of his mouth would be him begging me to fuck him into the next century, but instead, he said, "There's something else."

I stopped kissing him, but didn't feel like separating my body from his again.

"I don't know if it's a cause or an effect, but every single wave so far," he paused to take a deep breath, "you've breached my womb."

My brow flew up. "And that's unusual?"

Phillip turned his head slightly, looking deliciously bashful. "That's part of day two of instruction, but yes, it's extraordinarily unusual." He looked back up at me and said, "In a standard heat, an omega's womb will remain unbreachable. It opens enough to let sperm in, which is why an omega can get pregnant by any alpha, not just a bonded mate."

"But it's different when there's a bond?" I asked, already knowing the answer. A few things about Phillips behavior at the climax of the three previous waves suddenly made sense.

"When there's a bond, an omega's womb opens right up, allowing direct penetration from the bonded alpha." He paused, then blushed hard and said, "It feels incredible. Beyond any other type of orgasm. It's...it's indescribable."

"Yeah, it is," I said, breathless and flushed myself. "Now I know what that was."

"You could feel it?" he asked, sweet hope in his eyes.

"Fuck, yeah, I could feel it," I growled, showing my alpha particularly hard. "It was like sticking my dick directly into an electrical socket of pleasure."

Phillip laughed loudly, which caused his whole body to undulate. "I'll have to use that analogy in my next class too."

"Seriously," I said. "It felt like I plugged into something that short-circuited my entire body with pleasure. I didn't think I would ever stop coming."

Phillip grew serious again. "It's a good thing I'm on the pill, then," he said. "Because pregnancy is almost guaranteed from just one orgasm like that." He paused, swallowed, panted a bit, and said, "We had three. Even bonded pairs don't necessarily experience that during every single heat wave."

I felt like he'd given me some sort of amazing compliment. It also made me grin.

"Is your slutty omega womb trying to force me to get you pregnant?" I asked, laughing.

"Yes, I think so," Phillip laughed along with me. His expression changed again, and he said, "But I'm not looking to have kids right now. I mean, someday, yes, but not right now. I have too much going on."

"Me too, sweetheart," I said, bending down to kiss him again. "Someday, yes, but not right now." I kissed him again and said, "But if your body wants to tease and tempt mine and shoot omega electricity straight into my soul through my cock like that over and over, I won't complain."

"I won't complain either," Phillip panted, parting his legs and tilting his hips up. I could feel the heat and wetness of his slick against my balls as he writhed. "Those orgasms." He moaned like a dirty whore, like *my* dirty whore.

"Yeah," I said, knowing exactly what he meant and knowing he could feel that I knew it. "But someday." I bent down to kiss him, then continued with, "Someday I'm going to pump that hungry womb of yours so full that you'll conceive quadruplets."

He laughed, but as he looked up into my eyes, I could see the hope and the longing there. I could see that he knew I'd spoken the truth, and he accepted it as a truth he wanted. We were bonded, strange as it was, just like that.

"Oh, God," Phillip gasped. "You have to fuck me now. I need it. So badly. I need you in me now."

I laughed and kissed him, hands roving his body greedily, thinking, "Here we go again."

I could seriously get used to this heat thing.

Chapter Eight

Phillip

It was very possibly the best three days of my life. Jesse and I just clicked together. Whether it was ordinary compatibility or something more extraordinary, or maybe even supernatural, the sex was amazing. For once, I didn't feel completely self-conscious for acting like a depraved trollop as heat wave after heat wave hit me. I didn't sense a shred of judgement from Jesse, which was probably partially because he spent my whole heat behaving like an aggressive, sex-crazed maniac.

But all good things came to an end, including heat.

I knew it was over when I woke up on the morning of our fourth day together. Jesse and I were still snuggled together in bed, but as sleep left me, the prickling urge to get away rolled through me. I felt dirty and gross. The dried cum on my body and the leaking remnants of the last heat wave made me grimace in disgust instead of hum and smile and feel lucky for having such a virile alpha to take me through my heat. My asshole was sore as hell and throbbed with heat after being used so roughly for so long. Things inside weren't much better.

I did feel sated, though. As I woke up, I pushed myself away from Jesse and stretched on the empty, cool side of the mattress. Heat gaveth and heat tooketh away, or something like that. As disgusting as I felt on the outside, my insides were filled with a deep sense of satisfaction and completion. I knew I wasn't pregnant—omegas had that sixth sense and almost always knew if they'd conceived during their heat—but my body still thanked me for the good time by feeling warm and loose.

There was something else under the pulsing contentment, though, a sort of sadness, a feeling of regret. I'd never experienced that before. I'd walked away from all of my past heats—except the one I'd tried to tough out on my own with toys—feeling uplifted and self-satisfied. I'd always just thanked the alpha who had taken me through and gone on my merry way.

Something was different this time, but I couldn't put my finger on it.

I sat up, embarrassed by the gushing sensation in my ass, then threw my legs over the side of the bed.

"You up?" Jesse asked in a sleepy voice, stretching. He drew in a breath, then sniffed. "Your scent has changed."

"Yeah," I said, standing on slightly unsteady legs. "It's over."

I felt bad as I stepped away from the bed, guilty. I wasn't sure what it was all about. I was a progressive omega who was raised by forward-thinking parents. I had no qualms about sex and no guilt about having a trusted alpha I wasn't in a relationship with take me through. But when disappointment clouded Jesse's face as I walked away from the bed, heading to the bathroom, that guilty sadness within me deepened.

"I'm just going to take a shower," I said, my words a little stilted, as I glanced back at him. "I'll be quick so that you can get in once I'm done."

"Oh. Okay." Jesse sat up, looking a little lost in my messy bed.

"I'll just be a few minutes," I said, even though it was repetitive. I didn't know what else to say to him.

I rushed into the shower, self-conscious about being naked and leaky in front of him, self-conscious that I couldn't think of anything else to say, and self-conscious about all of the things I had said in the last few days. They all came back to me as I scrubbed spunk and dried slick off my body and out of my hair.

I'd told Jesse I loved him, and my whole body still throbbed with those feelings, but we hadn't even known each other a week. I'd felt him come all the way up inside me, inside my womb, but even though it was unusual, that degree of intimacy and pleasure wasn't unheard of. It had felt so significant at the time, but I recalled several of our ESAs reporting the same happening with some of their clients. Regular clients, yes, but clients all the same. The sex had been amazing, but maybe that was just how sex was supposed to be and I'd only ever had mediocre sex before?

The doubt that pressed down on me in the post-heat low was louder than thunder.

I finished rinsing my hair and stood with my face under the warm shower spray for a moment. It was the hormones. I knew damn well it was the hormones. When heat hormones flooded an omega's body, it was like a four-day high. When those levels evened out and returned to normal, omegas crashed. It was biology, nothing more.

So which feelings did I trust and which did I ignore? Were all those feelings of love and magic that I'd felt with Jesse during my heat real and the low I felt now just hormones, or was it the other way around? Was all that amped up affection and crazy-hot pleasure caused entirely by hormones that were now leaving my system so I could think clearly again?

I finished rinsing off, conscious of leaving enough hot water for Jesse, and got out of the shower. I dried quickly, then grabbed my toweling robe from its hook on the back of the bathroom door.

By the time I stepped out into the bedroom, Jesse had stripped the sheets off the bed and piled them near the door.

"I don't think you have any clean sheets left to remake the bed, but I could finish that load I started running the day before yesterday," Jesse said when he saw me. His voice had more uncertainty in it than I'd heard since he'd first addressed me in the classroom.

"Thanks," I said, walking over to my dresser, picking up several used wipes and the empty bottle of spermicide as I went. Also the plug, which had come in very handy on day three especially.

I had my back to him, but I heard Jesse breathing softly as he stood where he was. I could feel his stare on my back. I could practically hear him asking what he'd done wrong.

I'd just fished socks and underwear out of the top drawer when Jesse moved toward me. "You know, it was—"

He stopped when he came right up behind me and tried to put his hands on my arms. I couldn't stand the touch, and I wriggled away from him, putting space between us, as if he'd rushed toward me in an attack.

Instantly, I felt like an ass. "Sorry, sorry!" I said, turning to face him, shoulders slumping.

"No, I'm sorry," Jesse said, clearly upset and confused. "I didn't think you'd mind. I wasn't trying to be forward or anything, I just thought...."

We stared guiltily at each other for a moment. I felt horrible for rejecting his advances, and I knew, I just knew, that Jesse felt bad for unsettling me.

I let out a breath and forced myself to be logical. "It's the hormones," I said exactly what I'd been thinking in the shower. I cleared my throat, stood a little straighter and went on in my instructor voice. "We usually go over this toward the end of day two. As slutty as omegas get during heat, once it's over, we go through a period of recovery where we are averse to touch."

"You don't like to be touched after heat?" he asked, a faint glimmer of hope in his eyes.

"It's something all omegas experience," I explained, fighting to sound professional and not brokenhearted. "It's nature's way of ensuring that an omega completes the process of conception with their chosen mate before another alpha can swoop in and add a whole different load of sperm into the womb. And to avoid physical damage. I'm really sore back there right now."

"I guess that's a brilliant idea?" Jesse said, looking profoundly uncertain.

"Well, it makes sense. I'll give nature that," I said, trying to smile. I couldn't bear the awkwardness that settled over us from there, so I cleared my throat and said, "The water in the shower should still be warm."

Jesse stood where he was for a moment, radiating confusion. "Oh. I'll just go take a shower, then."

He stood there for a little while longer, though. The two of us stared at each other. I could still objectively see how attractive he was. Not attractive, smoking hot. Especially since he was still messy with dried cum and slick. The hair around his groin was particularly matted with it, which made my face burn with something a little like shame, but also a bit like pride. I'd turned him into a ravening beast who couldn't get enough of my ass.

Which was the problem. I'd turned him into that. My

heat, my scent, my hormones. That didn't mean it was all real, though.

"Okay, then," Jesse said at last, sucking in a breath, then turning to head to the bathroom.

"I'll make us some breakfast," I said, opening another drawer to take out a pair of baggy sweats, which were all my ass could handle touching it right about then. "Then we can talk about some of the things I usually teach on days three and four of the class. Hopefully your principal will be satisfied with everything, even though you didn't technically complete the training course."

"Oh, I think I was trained quite well," Jesse said with a grin as he disappeared into the bathroom.

I took a deep breath and relaxed a little. There were no hard feelings. Granted, there were feelings and I didn't know what they were, but at least Jesse was able to joke.

As the shower turned on, I slipped into the sweats and a modest shirt, then hurried out to the kitchen. I didn't want to be in the bedroom when Jesse came out again, especially if he was naked. It was one thing to walk around naked in front of each other during heat, but it didn't feel right now.

I was surprised when I glanced out through the kitchen window as I gathered stuff to make bacon and eggs to see a temporary bridge spanning the gap where the tree had taken out the old bridge. The new one was made of some sort of bright orange plastic and was clamped to the broken ends of the old bridge on either side of the ravine. It looked stable and sturdy, but I would feel much better when the old bridge could be rebuilt.

More importantly, the temporary bridge was a sure sign that people had been around my cabin while Jesse was taking me through my heat. That thought had me flushing with embarrassment. I searched for my phone, finding it in the living room, though I didn't remember how it got there, and checking to see if my parents had called.

Sure enough, I had a few missed calls and a text from Dad.

"*Just checking to see how things are going*," the text read. "*No need to reply. See you when you're done.*"

I blew out a breath and dialed my dad.

"The happy couple emerges at last," Dad answered the phone, sounding downright giddy.

"If by that you mean my heat is over, you're right," I said, walking back into the kitchen with my phone between my ear and shoulder.

"So? How was it?" Papa's voice sounded as Dad put the call on speaker.

"I hope you two are at home or in your office and not in the classroom building or anywhere people can overhear us," I told them, sounding peevish to my own ears.

"Poor baby," Papa said. "You've got post-heat blues, don't you."

I thought about denying it or arguing, but I decided just to sigh and admit it. "Yeah, a little. A little bit worse than ever before, if I'm honest."

"That happens when you've had a particularly good heat," Dad said.

"How do you know if I've had a particularly good heat?" I asked, dreading the answer.

"I was, er, up there helping the crew with the bridge replacement the day before yesterday," Dad said. "I knocked and then stepped in to see how you were getting along. You and Mr. Armstrong were definitely getting along."

I cringed. My dad had walked into my home in the middle of a heat wave on my peak day of heat. God only knew what he'd heard.

Then again, if anyone would know how to make sense of the conflicting things I felt, it would be Dad and Papa.

"Hey, have you guys ever felt, you know, really connected during a heat?" I asked. "Like, in the early days, before you were as deeply in love as you are now."

I heard them both chuckle, which I resented more than a little.

"Honey, your dad and I fell in love hard right from the start," Papa said, his voice soft. "It could have been the heat hormones helping things along, or it could have just been the fact that we were perfect for each other."

"And we still are," Dad said in a soppy voice.

I heard the two of them kiss as I cracked an egg into the frying pan, and I grimaced. Just because Papa was past heat age didn't mean he and Dad didn't get it on way too often for old people.

"Maybe I should let the two of you go now," I said, tending to the eggs as they fried. "It sounds like you're about to get up to something I really don't want to listen to."

"You're not the only one who gets to have fun," Dad said. He chuckled, then added, "We'll let you go. I'm sure you and Jesse have a lot to talk about this morning. Take your time getting back down to the complex. Ty's been doing just fine with your class, and they'll be done by noon."

"Thanks, Dad," I said.

I'd taken the phone away from my shoulder to hang up when Papa said, "Was there something else you wanted to talk about, Philly? You sound like you have something else on your mind."

I did. I still wanted answers about which of my emotions were real and which were hormones. But I heard Jesse step out of the bedroom, and a moment later, he appeared in the doorway of the kitchen, washed, dressed, and looking good.

"I'll ask about it all later," I said. "You two go have fun. And thanks for the bridge."

"We'll see you soon," Papa said.

I ended the call and set the phone on the table as Jesse came all the way into the room.

"That looks delicious," he said, coming all the way over to the stove. He almost rested a hand on my back before I tensed. "Sorry, I forgot for a second," he said with a sad look, taking a step away. He rolled his shoulders a little, as if to clear the faux pas from the air then said, "I feel like I could eat a horse right now."

"God, I hope not," I said, trying to keep it light myself. "I like horses."

"So do I." His smile came back, and he turned it on me with a blast of affection.

But was it real affection or just my hormones working their way out of his system?

"I'm making way more than I could usually eat," I explained, falling back into teacher mode. "This was another thing we were going to discuss on day two. Alphas and omegas both end up depleted after heat. You'll probably find that you're ravenously hungry for a couple of days. Don't worry about eating too much. Post-heat is not the time for a diet. Alphas and omegas both need all the calories they can get to replenish, particularly if the omega is pregnant."

Jesse's expression turned alarmed. "You aren't pregnant, are you? We took precautions. You're on the pill. All that spermicide. And how would you know? Isn't it too early?"

An uncomfortable pang of guilt, like I'd let Jesse down by not conceiving, attempted to swallow me before I could fight it off. Hormones. Again with the hormones.

"I'm not," I said as dispassionately as I could. "Omegas know when they've been impregnated from the moment of conception. If I had gotten pregnant during heat, the heat would have ended instantly, even if it was only the first wave. This heat definitely didn't end after one wave."

"Tell me about it," Jesse said, rolling his eyes and moving

to the fridge to take out some orange juice, helping me with breakfast. I thought it was unbearably sweet of him. "But I know what you're talking about. I had this beta classmate in middle school who used to brag to us all that his parents conceived him during the first heat wave of his mom's first heat. He was one of those conservative, purity culture types, and he insisted that he was almost a virgin birth, so we should all kiss the ground he walked on."

"Betas," I sniffed, shaking my head.

He laughed, and it was nice that we could share the joke, but something was still off.

I tried once more to handle it by engaging fully in teacher mode.

"I really don't want you to take it personally that I don't want you, or anyone else, touching me right now," I said, sliding the eggs onto a plate once they were done and filling up the pan with as much bacon as would fit. "It's just biology. Heat is pure biology. Our hormones have been going nuts for the past few days, making us think and feel everything way more than we would have otherwise. It isn't clear thinking at all. And now I'm crashing." I sent him an apologetic smile.

"Crashing?" he asked.

I nodded, then sighed. "I'm feeling depressed and...and guilty," I explained. "But it's perfectly normal, so don't worry about it," I rushed to add.

"Of course, I worry about it," Jesse said in a quiet, uncertain voice. He swayed toward me for a moment, then backed off. "I mean, if the whole point of this is for me to learn how to relate to my omega students and what they will experience in their lives, then of course I need to be concerned about it. I need to come up with ways to counsel both my omega and my alpha students about emotional and physical challenges they might face in the future."

"Right," I said, agreeing with his reasons for taking the training so seriously.

"But what do you mean you feel guilty?" he asked, leaning against the counter as I poked at the cooking bacon. He crossed his arms. "Do you feel guilty for...being so enthusiastic?"

I flushed with embarrassment, then shook my head. "No, I know this doesn't make any sense, considering what we talked about in terms of wanting children, but I feel guilty for not getting pregnant."

"Phillip, you don't have to worry about that," he said, his voice so soft and caring that tears welled in my eyes without warning.

"Oh, I know," I said with a little too much cheer, rubbing my face to fight the tears. "Like I said, it's hormones. My emotions right now aren't real. I doubt they've been real for the last few days."

I regretted saying that as soon as the words passed my lips. Jesse looked devastated.

Which shocked me. He couldn't feel the same as I thought I maybe felt, could he? Maybe it was real after all, for both of us?

Post-heat blues sucked.

Before I could latch onto the hope that our emotions had been real after all, Jesse shrugged and pushed away from the counter. "Yeah, we'll get over it, right?"

"We will," I insisted. It felt like a lie.

"I'm looking forward to getting back to school on Monday and telling Winters and the staff all about this experience," he said, opening a cupboard to take down some mugs for coffee. "I mean, not the details, obviously," he said, face red. "Just the theory. I think it's important for teaching staff to know about these things."

"I certainly think so," I said, heart sinking as he moved

farther away from me. "This will be done in just a second," I said.

"Good, because I'm starving," he said, pouring himself a cup of coffee.

He'd said the same thing already. Our conversation was going in circles. It was completely awkward, and I didn't know what to do about it.

I couldn't do anything about anything, though. All I could do was make breakfast, ride out the wave of post-heat hormones, and hope that I'd be able to put my life back together after the most momentous few days of my life.

Jesse

I stopped trying to figure out what I was feeling by the time we were halfway through breakfast. Everything felt so wrong. I sat across the table from Phillip, listening but not listening to him talking about the details of what the ESA training class learned on the third and fourth days. From the sound of things, I'd covered all of it in the last few, mind-blowing days Phillip and I had spent together. And then some.

"So basically," Phillip finally finished up once our breakfast plates were empty and we'd each had a second cup of coffee, "the ESA trainees go through a heat wave simulation at the end of the class. They don't actually have sex with the instructors and examiners," he quickly qualified. "They just go through the procedures, asking the consent questions, and then talking through the steps they would take if they were with an actual omega in heat."

"Those consent questions are nice, but the process takes

too long," I said, trying not to sound critical, but unable to stop myself. The irritated feeling I'd had when I'd first arrived at the institute was back, but now it was hyper-focused on Phillip particularly.

He shouldn't have been sitting with a table between us. He should have been sitting on my lap. Which was a ridiculous thought, since he was a grown man and not a toddler. And I knew that his post-heat hormones made it so that he didn't want anyone touching him, but I still wanted to be near him. Nearer than across a table.

"Things usually haven't progressed to the point where we were when the questions are asked," Phillip informed me with a frown. "It's my fault for ignoring the signs and thinking my heat wouldn't come until the end of the week." He paused, brow knitting in confusion as he fiddled with his fork. "I always know when my heat is coming. I've never gotten it wrong before. Omegas usually have a full day's warning before things get like that. It gives them plenty of time to call for an ESA and to go through the procedures."

His frown made me want to take him in my arms and soothe him, let him know everything would be alright, that it wasn't his fault, that he was wonderful and beautiful and perfect.

Those thoughts tipped my emotions even more off-balance. Hadn't we just gone through the whole thing about how what we were feeling wasn't real? How it was just the hormones?

Hormones sucked, and I would never trust them again. I hated not being able to trust my own feelings. I was an alpha, I liked certainty and command. Yes, that was a cliché, but clichés had their roots in the truth. I didn't like not trusting my inner self.

"Either way," I said, getting up and picking up my plate with one hand, "this has been a really interesting experience for me." Not to mention the best sex of my life by a factor of a thousand.

Phillip stood as well, but I took his plate when he tried to reach for it.

For a moment, our fingers brushed. It was like we were both electric and a spark arced between us. Phillip sucked in a breath, his gaze snapping up to meet my eyes. I couldn't read the look he gave me...except that I knew what he was thinking anyhow. That spark between us wasn't insignificant, and it puzzled him.

I wanted so desperately to trust that it was something, that what I'd felt during Phillip's heat was real. I still felt it in my gut like it was real, it was just my damn head that second-guessed everything now.

"Do you think the training class is still in progress?" I said, heading into the kitchen and keeping things casual. "Or do you think everyone will have left by now?"

Phillip grabbed the coffee mugs and a stray fork and spoon and followed me into the kitchen. He glanced at the clock on the microwave and said, "They're probably just finishing up. If we...if we head down there now, we might still be able to catch them to say goodbye."

He was still frowning as he spoke, like leaving our little heat bubble wasn't what he wanted to do at all.

But again, I was half convinced that was just my imagination. That or wishful thinking.

If he gave me any sign that what we'd felt was real, I would drop everything and do whatever he needed me to do to stay with him.

That thought hit me like a surprise left jab. I shook my head to push it out of my head as I rinsed our plates, then handed them to Phillip to put in the dishwasher. I couldn't just drop my life for a man I'd met four days ago...could I?

"I can imagine that even a practice scenario for the new

ESA trainees doesn't quite prepare them for the real thing," I said with a sideways smirk for him.

Phillip answered with a distracted smile and a half laugh, "We try to send newbie alphas to experienced omegas who have used our services before. Because you're right, that first time for an ESA can be overwhelming. We always do a debriefing after an ESA's first visit so we can answer any questions that might have come up, and we require ESAs to file a report after each call. No sordid details, mind you, just a record of how things went so that we can better match up alphas and omegas in the future."

"And I suppose you ask your omegas to rate the alphas, like they've just finished reading a book and should leave a review," I said, my grin a little more genuine.

"Oh, of course," Phillip said. "Reviews are essential. They're how we assess whether we're doing a good job and providing the very best service for our clients."

I shouldn't have asked, but I had to. "And how would you rate me?"

Phillip's awkwardness melted into a bashful smile that had my blood pumping again. "Five stars," he said, a blush painting his cheeks.

I closed the dishwasher and leaned against the counter, crossing my arms. "Not 'one star, too much sex'?"

Phillip laughed out loud. "There's no such thing as too much sex."

"You've got that right, sweetheart," I said, winking at him.

For a moment, just a moment, everything was perfect. My whole body, not just my heart, throbbed with affection for Phillip. For just a moment, I knew that everything I'd felt had been real. Crazy as it sounded, I'd found my soulmate. I was happy, bursting with confidence, ready to take on the world and bend over backwards to protect and cherish Phillip with everything I had. I could feel a corresponding vibration in

Phillip as well. That spark we'd felt at the table continued to arc between us, connecting us and making us warm, inside and out.

A second later, and the feeling was muddled again as Phillip lost his smile and turned away.

He heaved a sigh and said, "We really need to get back to the classroom building. I'd ask if you have all your things, but you didn't bring anything up here, so there's nothing to take away."

Those words felt like a dagger in my heart. Was he saying I should just walk away, because I didn't have anything real to stick around for?

"Yeah, good thing, right?" I laughed, feigning casualness as we walked out of the kitchen and headed for the cabin door. "I bet you're eager to get back to your normal life too and to have your home and your body back."

Phillip darted a quick, almost dispirited, sideways glance to me. I could feel disappointment rippling off him, but he said, "Yeah, something like that."

I changed the subject as soon as we were outside the cabin with, "That temporary bridge looks surprisingly sturdy."

"We've had to put things like this up before," Phillip said as we crossed the bridge. "This mountain has a great location and magnificent views, not to mention exactly the sort of privacy for what we do here, but there are several ravines like this separating a couple of distinct parts of the mountain."

He went on to explain more about the physical features of the mountain, the reason why his parents had bought the property thirty years before, and the engineering wonders that had been performed to make more and more of the mountain habitable over time. I was impressed with everything Bangers & Mash had accomplished, and not just in terms of architecture. I understood the ESA program so much better now.

I understood that it took an alpha with a strong personality and self-control to walk away from the sort of experience I'd just had with Phillip without feeling like he'd left a piece of his soul behind.

"Oh look! The lovebirds emerge," Mr. Mash greeted us as Phillip and I entered the classroom building. He and Phillip's dad were in the middle of putting up some sort of display on one of the long corkboards that stretched the length of one wall.

"Phillip, Mr. Armstrong," Mr. Banger greeted us with a pretend solemn nod. His eyes glittered with humor, though. "I take it a good time was had by all?"

"I am very impressed with your son," I said with a respectful nod. "He is an excellent teacher and made me feel comfortable the whole time."

I could feel Phillip's embarrassment radiating from him. "Jesse was attentive and considerate and respected me at all times," he said.

"That's my review, I guess," I said to him with a sideways look.

Phillip broke into a laugh, his cheeks flaring an even brighter shade of pink. When he glanced at me, I felt that spark between us again.

I wanted to touch him, to take his hand. I wanted to do more than that. I wanted to pull him into my arms and repeat all the confessions of love I'd made in the height of passion. Phillip was mine now, dammit. It was an archaic thought, and I was a little ashamed of those possessive, cliché alpha feelings, but it felt so right to feel that way.

Until I inched slightly toward Phillip, reaching subtly for his hand, and he took a large step away.

"Is my class still going?" he asked, walking away from me to peek into the classroom we'd used the other day. "How did Ty do?"

Phillip's parents exchanged a knowing look and took their

time answering. I had the strange feeling they were laughing at us.

"Ty did fine," Mr. Mash said going back to tacking motivational material to the board. "It isn't his first rodeo, you know. He's taught training classes on his own before."

"When he's not out on calls," Mr. Banger added. He looked at me and said, "Ty is one of our finest ESAs. He's very experienced. If you have any questions, you can talk to him."

Prickles raced down my back as I tried to figure out what he meant by that.

"I don't know if that would be appropriate," I said. "I wasn't here to train as an ESA, just to do a little continuing education for my teaching job."

"That's right," Mr. Mash said, as though connecting some dots. "You're a teacher too. Huh. You and Phillip have a lot in common." He grinned like he'd said we were most definitely soulmates and I shouldn't even think about leaving.

Or maybe that feeling came from Phillip himself as he glanced anxiously between his papa and me.

Either way, unless Phillip told me flat-out that he had feelings for me and not just hormones, it didn't matter. I had a life to get back to.

"Do you have any sort of graduation ceremony or final speech that you give to your trainees once they make it through the program?" I asked, trying to sound professional and cool.

"Not exactly," Mr. Banger said handing his husband another poster for the corkboard. "We do final consultations with each trainee after the simulations are done to let them know how they did and where they could improve, and then we discuss scheduling and make their first appointment with a regular client."

"Dad and Papa have the whole training program ticking

like a well-oiled machine at this point," Phillip said, stepping over to stand near his fathers.

"I can tell," I said. "I'm really impressed. And thank you." I looked specifically to Phillip, hoping he would hear more than my words. "Thank you for everything."

"You're welcome," Phillip said with an uncertain smile.

I'd hoped he would say, "My pleasure," so that I could make a joke and lighten the bristling tension between us, but he didn't.

I couldn't think of any other reasons to stick around. I wasn't part of the class anymore, I'd had the ultimate practicum for the experience, and now it was over. It was still early, so if I wanted to, I could go to the beach and spend the day lounging in the sun, swimming in the ocean, and maybe hitting a bar or two to meet other omegas. I should have felt infinitely more confident approaching omegas after this weekend. I knew so much more about them now.

But I didn't want another omega. I didn't know about omegas in general, I knew about Phillip. I knew the way his scent magnified until I felt like I was in a peach orchard when his heat started. I knew the plaintive sounds he made when he was so horny he couldn't think straight. I knew the heat of his skin under my lips and the taste of his slick. I knew what it felt like to empty my soul directly into his womb and to feel like the two of us were one person.

I realized then that I was staring at Phillip and that the hallway was silent. Embarrassment washed through me, and I cleared my throat.

"Well, um, I'm just going to go back to the dorm room I didn't use to get my things, then I should probably head out," I said to Phillip's parents.

My eyes went straight back to Phillip, though, like he was the magnet in my compass. I just needed one sign from him that it had all been real, just one.

Phillip cleared his throat and thrust his hands in his pockets. "I'll walk you over to the dorm, then down to your car."

He crossed past me, heading for the door.

That was it then. It had all been a dream. Fucking hormones. I hated having my heart toyed with. The worst thing was, unlike my break-up with Greg, I couldn't blame anyone in this situation. I couldn't blame anyone but myself for wanting to believe in fairy tales.

It didn't take long to fetch my things. I hadn't actually unpacked on that first day. Most of my things were still in my overnight bag, which sat undisturbed on the bed in the room that had been assigned to me. All I had to do was grab it and my car keys where I'd left them on the dresser, then head out and down the hill to the parking lot.

Phillip and I didn't talk about anything important as we made the journey. In fact, by the time we reached my car, I couldn't remember anything we'd talked about at all. I could only feel anxious and desperate for any indication from Phillip that I shouldn't go.

I didn't get it as we reached my car. I didn't get it when I opened the door to the back and tossed my bag in. I didn't even get it when I shut that door and opened the driver's door.

"Well," I said, letting the word hang in the air.

"Well," Phillip echoed.

We stood there just staring at each other. Desperation pulsed through me, but I was an alpha, I was supposed to be strong and proud. I couldn't break down and drop to my knees, begging Phillip to tell me he actually loved me and he hadn't just been in a hormonal haze. It was his heat and his hormones that had turned me around. I needed him to be the one to tell me to stay.

"Traffic shouldn't be too bad," Phillip said instead. "It's a nice day for the beach."

Was that a hint? Was he telling me to get lost?

"Yeah," I said with a casual shrug. "I might go down there and take a walk before going back to my normal life."

"So, you're eager to get back to normal?" he asked, eyes glittering a little. Hopefully not with tears.

Unless that was my imagination too.

"Of course," I said with a shrug. "I need to figure out how to integrate this experience into my teaching strategy."

"Oh, yes, of course," Phillip said. He paused, then added, "Don't let me keep you."

My heart sank. He didn't want to keep me. Fuck.

"Take care of yourself, okay?" I swayed closer to him, like I would kiss him goodbye, but changed my mind. He would recoil from the touch, post-heat, and I didn't think I could stand being rejected again.

"Okay, you too," Phillip said. He smiled and took a step back.

That was it. It was over. I smiled in return and slipped into my car, but I felt terrible. It was ten times worse than breaking up with Greg. I felt like I'd lost something far more precious, like a limb.

I shut the door and turned the car on. "Bye," I said, desperate to say one last thing to the man who had changed every cell in my body and tipped my world on its head.

"Bye," Phillip repeated, stepping back to the curb and waving.

I rolled up the car window and backed out of the space. I wanted to cry, but those emotions felt false, like I shouldn't be feeling them at all. I couldn't make any sense of it as I turned and started driving to the end of the parking lot and the long, winding drive that would take me off the mountain.

Every second I drove away from him made me feel like I was driving into blackness and despair.

Chapter Ten

Phillip

Headaches, body aches, and anxiety were not supposed to be part of the post-heat funk. My body hadn't gotten the memo, evidently. I stood glued to my spot, watching Jesse's car leave the parking lot, then turn the corner that took him out of sight. My head throbbed horribly when I lost sight of him.

That was it. He was gone. The whole thing was over.

I'd waited and waited for him to say something that would indicate he wanted to stay, that the things he'd said to me in the heat of, well, heat were true. I knew all about hormones, knew I couldn't trust my own feelings or reactions, but Jesse was an alpha. He was the one who would have a better handle on whether what had passed between us was real or not.

But he'd said nothing, and now there I was, standing in a parking lot, staring at nothing.

I growled, pressed my fingertips to my temples, then turned to plod my way back to the classroom building. I didn't really want to be around anyone. I didn't want anyone coming near me, except Jesse. I didn't want anyone to touch me, except maybe Jesse. I didn't want to eat anything, unless Jesse had made it. And I didn't want to talk to anyone, except Jesse.

"Sweetheart, you don't look so good," Papa said as soon as I stepped back into the classroom building.

I nearly burst into tears. Jesse had called me "sweetheart", and it had felt like the most wonderful word in the world. Hearing it from Papa's lips, even though he was my papa, was close to sacrilege.

"I'm fine," I said without thinking about it. I slumped against the wall, rubbing my temples even harder. Actually, I felt as though I was in the process of being pulled through a wringer.

"Jesse left?" Dad asked, one eyebrow raised halfway as he looked at me from the top of the stepladder he was using to hang a mobile from the ceiling.

I nodded, but I didn't feel like talking at that moment.

"He seems really nice," Papa said, also watching me as he tacked something to the board.

I knew it was a leading question. I knew there was much more to what Papa was asking with that statement.

The trouble was, I didn't know what to say about it. I wasn't some teenager with his first, disappointed crush, but I still felt like I needed my Papa or I might crumble.

"Hmm." Dad's hum as he stepped down from the ladder had me dragging my head up to look at him. He wore a look of concern, but there was a very Dad-like sparkle in his eyes. "Interesting." He walked all the way over to me and crossed his arms, tapping his chin, like he was looking at some sort of scientific specimen. "Very, very interesting."

I sighed as I tried to stand straighter and face him. It felt like my body had been slammed with a two-by-four repeatedly. "Could we skip this part, please?" I asked. "I don't really feel up to probing questions about my heat from my parents."

"So, it was good, then," Dad said. It wasn't a question.

I sighed. "Really good. Best I've ever had." I had no idea why I was being so honest about something so intimate with my dad.

Papa caught on to something happening, finished with the poster he was tacking up, then rushed over to join us. He put a hand to my forehead the way he had when I was a sick kid. I flinched away.

"No touching right now, Papa," I scolded him. "You know how it is post-heat."

"I do know how it is," Papa said, glancing to Dad with a giddy grin. "I have questions about other things, though."

"What other things?" I said, rubbing my temples some more. The headache was getting worse, like something inside me was stretching and stretching to the point where it would break.

Papa rested his weight on one hip and crossed his arms in an imitation of Dad. "Does it feel like you know what he's thinking, even when he doesn't say anything?" he asked. "Or was there ever a moment when you thought you heard him say something when he didn't actually speak?"

I sucked in a breath and my eyes went wide for a moment.

Then I frowned and shook my head, slumping against the wall again.

"People don't bond that fast, Papa," I said, closing my eyes. "And the whole fated mates thing is just a myth."

"But you have a headache now, don't you?" Dad asked. "Body aches? Feels like you've been hit by a truck?"

I opened one eye, even though the light made my head throb, and frowned at Dad. "It has to be hormones," I said. "The day after heat is always unpredictable. I'll be fine in a couple of hours. I just need a nap or something."

Dad and Papa exchanged excited smiles.

"It is hormones," Papa said slowly. "And it is part of the post-heat low."

"Why didn't you ever tell me about this, then?" I asked, feeling like someone was attaching more and more weights to my body with each passing moment. "This is the kind of thing I should be teaching about. It's never been like this before. Is it something I did? Something Jesse and I did during my heat waves?"

I suddenly thought of all the other things that had never happened to me before during heat waves, but that had happened with Jesse. Like the way my entire body had just opened up and begged for him. Like the mind-melting orgasms that came from him penetrating my womb. Like the very fact that my womb opened up for him like it was a hungry whore. Every. Single. Time.

"Oh, it definitely has to do with Jesse," Papa said, smirking.

I didn't have the patience for his teasing. "Yes, we were very physically compatible," I confessed. It was horrifically embarrassing to admit these sorts of things to my parents, but I said, "My womb accepted him. Every time."

Papa gasped in delight and looked to Dad, who was beaming.

"It's not the first time that's happened to me," I said, trying to cut what I knew Papa was thinking off before he could get started. "The whole womb thing happened one other time too."

"During every wave or just one wave during a single heat?" Dad asked.

I grudgingly admitted, "Just the one wave. One time."

"But it happened every time with Jesse," Dad said to clarify.

I nodded.

Dad and Papa exchanged another look.

"Son, what are you standing here for?" Papa asked, incredulous. "Why did you let your soulmate just walk out of here and drive away?"

"He's not my soulmate," I said loudly, pushing away from the wall. It felt like I was lying, and my whole body heated with guilt as I went on. "I barely know Jesse. He showed up four days ago and got under my skin from the very start. Yes, the sex was spectacular, but that has to just be biology, right? Whatever genetic markers he has match really well with mine. That's why the entire heat was so explosive."

"We raised him better than this," Papa told Dad.

I didn't appreciate his teasing or the way the two of them seemed to think the whole thing was a joke.

"I know what you're going to say," I snapped, a little too loudly, but God, my head was pounding. "You're going to say we bonded, that we're mates. But bonding doesn't happen with strangers, it happens when people have been together and in love for years. It happens when people know each other. You two had been married for years before you bonded, right?"

Dad shook his head. "Actually, no. Your papa and I bonded during the first wave of his first heat."

"And we'd only been dating for a week," Papa said.

I blinked at the two of them. "But you went to school together, right? You'd known each other for years."

"From afar," Dad said. "I'd been aware of your papa for a while, but I didn't work up the nerve to talk to him until we were in college."

That surprised me. Dad was the most confident, self-assured alpha I knew. I could hardly imagine him having a hard time talking to anyone, let alone Papa.

"I was too shy to approach him myself, but I didn't realize

we were meant to be together until that first heat wave," Papa said.

"But that's my point," I argued. "You knew each other. Jesse and I were virtual strangers when my heat started. So what if it was amazing and if we spent half the time telling each other we were in love. It was the hormones."

Dad and Papa exchanged another look. "You told each other you loved each other?" Papa asked.

"Yes?" I suddenly wasn't certain that was normal after all. "But that's just what heat hormones do, right?"

"Heat hormones make you amorous and affectionate," Papa said. "They make you want to have your brains fucked out."

"Papa," I muttered, hot with embarrassment. He was my papa, for Christ's sake. I did not want to hear about him having his brains fucked out.

Papa ignored me. "Heat hormones do not force you to fall in love with the alpha taking you through heat. If they did, we would have to train a new ESA every time we sent one out on a call."

"Bonding, on the other hand," Dad said, "heightens the feelings of love that you already have. Being bonded to the omega you're taking through heat makes it almost impossible not to tell them you love them every three seconds."

"But we aren't bonded," I insisted, frustrated that they weren't getting my point.

My head still throbbed, but at least it wasn't as bad as it had been moments ago. Which felt like it proved my point. I was already getting over Jesse.

Which was the most depressing thing I'd ever felt in my life. It couldn't be true. It wasn't happening. I loved him. We were meant to—

I stopped myself and shook my head. "It takes time to bond. There's no such thing as love at first sight."

"There absolutely is," Papa insisted.

"And even if it's not love at first sight, it's something," Dad said. "There are all kinds of documented cases of alphas and omegas bonding immediately, then getting to know each other later. Those are some of the happiest relationships I've ever heard of."

I started to say something, but Dad continued over me with, "You're always teaching about biology. Well, this is biology too. Sometimes biology knows immediately what it wants and the heart and mind have to play catch-up."

"You and Jesse Armstrong are obviously perfect for each other," Papa picked up where Dad left off. "Your bodies know it. Your hearts probably know it too. You're both just letting your heads get in the way. You let him walk away, but he wasn't savvy enough to demand to stay."

"Which should be an indicator that we didn't bond, we're not fated mates," I argued.

"Did you tell him how you're feeling?" Dad asked. "Were you open with him about the things you're feeling? Or did you try to dismiss them and explain them away?"

I froze, blinking at nothing, as I ran over our conversation in my head. I sort of had dismissed everything as hormones. I'd tried to be all clinical and teacher-y and explain instead of talking about how I felt.

Had Jesse tried to tell me what he was feeling? Had I dismissed him or given him indications that I didn't feel the same way?

I'd pushed him away and told him I didn't want to be touched. That was a normal post-heat reaction, but did Jesse know that? He'd never been with an omega in heat before. He'd never experienced the highs or the lows. He very easily could have thought I was letting him down gently, and then he could have been stand-offish, thinking I didn't want him.

"Oh my God," I said, rubbing my hands over my face. "I think we bonded."

"See?" Papa said, though he was looking at Dad, not me. "I told you."

"You were right," Dad said with a sigh. He drew Papa into his arms and kissed him. "You're always right. I should have learned that by now."

"You should have," Papa said, kissing him back.

"What do I do?" I interrupted their love fest, falling into a panic fest of my own. "I let him walk away. I let him leave the mountain."

"We have his address in the office, you know," Dad said.

Papa peeled away from him and headed to the office door. "Go get in your car and I'll send the address to your phone."

"Thanks, Papa," I said, dashing for the door.

I ran outside and down the path that led to the parking lot as fast as I could go with my body feeling like I'd fallen off the mountain and hit every ravine on the way down. Already, I was feeling better. Just making the decision to go after Jesse had the headache lifting and my body moving with more coordination.

It could have been that, or it could have been something else.

As I made it to the parking lot, just about the time I realized I didn't have my car keys with me, I spotted Jesse's car rounding the corner and speeding back into the parking lot.

He'd come back.

I burst into wild laughter, my heart lifting. Without a care for anything else, I sprinted into the parking lot, ignoring the cars, and raced straight to the spot where Jesse had stopped his car and turned it off. The door flew open and he leapt out.

"I couldn't do it," he said, his voice loud and booming and filled with affection. "I got to the bottom of the mountain, but I just couldn't do it. I felt horrible, like I'd been beat up.

But as soon as I turned around and headed back, the pain started to lift."

"I know," I said, running to him and throwing myself into his arms. "I felt it too."

That was all I was able to get out before Jesse closed his arms around me and lifted me clean off my feet so that he could kiss me.

It was the best kiss I'd ever had. Better even than during heat. Jesse had come back. He loved me after all. Our mouths were hungry for each other, and we each made desperate, needy sounds as our lips crushed together and our tongues danced and tasted. It felt so good to be molded against him, enfolded and cared for, that I didn't even stop to think I should have been recoiling from his touch post-heat. It was Jesse's touch, Jesse's kiss. How could I ever recoil from that?

"I love you," Jesse said, panting. He set me on my feet and grasped my face with both hands. "I love you, and it's not hormones, it's not just heat. It's real. It's what I really, actually feel. And no one can tell me otherwise. Maybe you don't feel the same—"

"I do," I said, panting and laughing and feeling as though my heart might beat right out of my chest. "And you're right, it's not just hormones or heat. I love you, Jesse. It doesn't make sense, and I'm sure it's just the beginning, but I love you for real. I love you so much."

He scooped me into his arms to kiss me again, this time with a deep sense of satisfaction and relief. His body was big and warm around mine, making me feel like the most loved and protected man ever. It felt like coming home to where I was supposed to be.

I didn't know how long it was before we paused for breath, but once we did, I said, "Dad and Papa believe we bonded, that we're fated mates."

"I thought fated mates was a fairy tale," Jesse said, smiling from ear to ear and stroking the sides of my face with his thumbs.

"I officially believe in fairy tales," I said with a laugh. "And maybe it is just biology on steroids, but I don't care. I love you, so much, even if I barely know you. But I *do* know you," I insisted. "I know all the things that matter."

"Me too," Jesse said, beaming. "And I am really looking forward to learning all the rest of the things now too."

"God, it will be so wonderful," I said, throwing myself against him and leaning my head on his shoulder. "It will be magical to learn everything about you, knowing you're mine."

"It will be like opening a new treasure every day," Jesse said, hugging me tight. He laughed. "I thought I was coming up here to sit through a boring class, but I've learned so much more. And now I'm looking forward to you not only training me to be your perfect alpha, but to be your perfect mate."

His words were so beautiful that I burst into tears, squeezing him even closer. "I love you, Jesse Armstrong. And that is only going to get better and stronger every day."

"I love you too, sweetheart."

I breathed in his scent, our scents mingled together. Somehow, they just worked. They worked perfectly. We worked perfectly together.

I HOPE YOU ENJOYED JESSE AND PHILLIP'S STORY! And for those of you who are new to this genre, welcome to omegaverse! I fell in love with this crazy genre a while ago, and I just knew that I had to put my own spin on it. So here we are with Bangers & Mash! This is my light-hearted take on all things alpha/beta/omega, mate bonding, juicy heat fun, and true love. I hope you'll come along for the whole ride with all the other fun books I have planned.

Next up is Ty's story, *The Wrong Omega*. Tybalt Martin is one of Bangers & Mash's most senior Emergency Support Alphas and has an important role in the company's plans to expand to cities beyond Barrington. He loves his job and considers it his calling to help omegas. So when he goes on what he thinks will be a routine call and finds a young omega in extreme distress at the onset of his heat, he doesn't think twice about doing the job he was sent to do. Except that the unfortunate omega Ty takes to bed isn't the client after all. Winslow Hartwell is the wrong omega...and the bond that Ty unexpectedly forms with him could spell the end of his career.

Keep clicking to get started on Chapter One...

If you enjoyed this book and would like to hear more from me—as MM Farmer or my other identities, Merry Farmer (Historical Romance and more) or Em Farmer (Contemporary Romance) please sign up for my newsletter! When you sign up, you'll get your choice of a free, full-length novella. One choice is *A Passionate Deception*. It is an MF romance, but it has a strong MM secondary character, who gets his own book in my May Flowers series. Part of my West Meets East series, *A Passionate Deception* can be read as a stand-alone. Your other choice is *Rendezvous in Paris*. It is an MM Victorian story that is part of my *Tales from the Grand Tour* series, but can also be read as a standalone. Pick up your free copy today by signing up to receive my newsletter (which I only send out when I have a new release)!

Sign up here: http://eepurl.com/cbaVMH

Are you on social media? I am! Come and join the fun on Facebook: http://www.facebook.com/merryfarmerreaders

I'm also a huge fan of Instagram and post lots of original content there: https://www.instagram.com/merryfarmer/

And, oh gosh, I signed up for TikTok too! They never should have let me on there, but if you want to watch me embarrassing myself in videos, you can follow me here: https://www.tiktok.com/@merryfarmer

And now, get started on *The Wrong Omega*...

Ty

I was the best Emergency Support Alpha in the business. Thinking that wasn't any sort of arrogance on my part, it was a fact. I had been with Bangers & Mash for nearly ten years, since graduating from Barrington University with a degree in psychology *summa cum laude* and being recruited directly to work for B&M by Salazar Banger himself. I'd worked my way up from trainee ESA to Assistant Director in just five years, and in the last five, I'd not only helped teach training classes for new alphas to the program, I'd begun helping with plans to expand the business into other cities by setting up B&M branches along the east coast.

Which was why, even though I was on my way to meet a client, I answered when Sal Banger's name popped up on the dashboard screen of my Ranger as I headed into Barrington.

"Morning, boss," I answered the call, keeping my eyes on the road and my grip on the steering wheel tight. "Something wrong?"

"Morning, Ty. No, not at all," Sal said in the deep, alpha

rumble his voice always had. It made people think he was angry when actually, Sal Banger was one of the nicest guys I had ever met. "You headed off the mountain before I had a chance to talk to you about the trip next week."

I winced slightly, frustrated with myself for setting out on this latest ESA call in such a hurry. "Sorry," I said. "Nick told me everything was taken care of for the trip and that I could head out. This omega sounded pretty eager to meet. He thinks his heat is going to start any second now."

"Is this the young guy? The one in his second year of medical school who can't be bothered to date?" Sal asked.

I was tempted to laugh at that characterization, but to do so would have been crass. It was none of my business why omegas hired an ESA to take them through their heat instead of turning to a partner or a trusted friend. Omegas almost always knew when heat was coming, and most of the ones I had ever known were either dating an alpha—or occasionally a strong beta—who could take them through, or they had an alpha friend who was willing to help them out.

Of course, the entire reason Sal Banger and Nick Mash had founded B&M was for those omegas who either didn't have anyone or who wanted just to get on with it and have the three or four disruptive days of their heat taken care of by a professional so they could avoid emotional attachment and get on with their lives.

That, and B&M had been founded so less fortunate omegas wouldn't be forced to sell their heat in the back alleys or underground networks of people who sought to take advantage of young men and women when they were at their most vulnerable.

"Yep," I answered Sal's question. "Doyle Curry. He said his future career as a surgeon is everything to him, but he's worried about the stigma of heat in a profession that has traditionally been dominated by alphas and betas."

"Got it," Sal said. I could practically hear my boss nod on the other end of the call. "Well, good luck with him. You're meeting at The Grand, right?"

"Yep. Mr. Curry wanted a hotel instead of his residence, and the omega is always right."

Sal laughed. "Good. The Grand knows to charge the room to our account. I think Hamish is still there, recovering after his call the other day, so say hi if you see him."

"Will do," I said.

"Which brings me around to the purpose for my call," Sal went on, his tone shifting. "About this Norwalk trip next week."

"I'm looking forward to it," I said, cracking one of my rare smiles.

"Good," Sal said. "This expansion could be really good for us. Better still, it will be good for the omegas of Norwalk. Sanchez and Cross think so too."

Kevin Sanchez and his wife, Madeline Cross, were the financers who had pledged half the money needed to bring a B&M branch to Norwalk. The small industrial city was big enough to support a new B&M location, but didn't have the budget to fund it through tax dollars alone, but Sanchez and Cross had stepped up to donate the cash needed to make the new branch a reality. I'd been working with them through email and video calls for a while now, and was scheduled to head to Norwalk in a week to iron out the last details and to get everyone to sign on the dotted line.

It was a huge step for Norwalk, and a big one for me personally as well. It was the first time Sal and Nick had trusted me with something as big as masterminding the opening of a new B&M branch, and it definitely represented a step up in my career.

And my career was everything to me. It wasn't just a job, it was a passion.

"I just had word from Sanchez and Cross," Sal went on as I turned my truck off the highway and headed along the city street that would take me closer to the beach, where The Grand was located. "They've offered to have you stay at their house as opposed to in a hotel. Are you okay with that?"

"Yeah, sure," I said. I usually kept to myself when I was off the clock, especially if I was just coming off an ESA call, like I would be when I left for the trip. Omega hormones affected alphas too, even if I didn't have any deep emotional connection with my client. I usually took a few days off after calls, to unscramble my thoughts and return to equilibrium. But if the couple who wanted to donate that much money to build a branch wanted to entertain me for a few days personally, I wouldn't say no to it. I couldn't afford to with so much on the line.

"They sent around an itinerary as well," Sal said. "They've got you doing a tour of Norwalk which includes several sites they think would be good for an office, one of which is part of a special housing project they've spearheaded, and a meet-and-greet with the mayor and several town councilors. Does that work for you?"

"Anything you want, boss," I said. "You know my first and only priority is to B&M. I believe in the company, and I'm happy to see it expand."

"That's what I like to hear," Sal said, and I could hear a smile in his voice. "You're one of the best we've got, Ty. I don't know how we would manage without you."

I smiled again. Twice in one hour. It must have been a record. "Thank, boss," I said. "And whatever it takes to get this new branch sorted, just let me know, and I'll do it."

"We'll have one last meeting in a few days, after your call," Sal said. "Until then, enjoy your call."

"Thanks, Sal."

I ended the call, feeling confident and looking forward to

the trip next week. I shook my head a bit over the way Sal always told me to enjoy my ESA calls. I wasn't there to enjoy myself, I was there for the omega. Sure, taking an omega through heat was pleasurable. Heat sex was wildly good for both the alpha and the omega. Too many of my buddies liked to tease me about how lucky I was to be able to bang omegas in heat multiple times a month.

I didn't see it that way. I had a duty of care to the omegas who hired an ESA for their heat. They always had a sensitive reason why they wanted a professional for such an intimate encounter, and I had vowed ten years ago when I received my ESA license that I would always respect their reasons and their needs, particularly when they wanted to keep those reasons to themselves. It wasn't my place to question any omega, just to help them.

The Grand was located right along Barrington's busiest stretch of beach. It was centrally located in the seaside town, which meant the area and the hotel itself saw a lot of traffic, but the hotel was unfailingly discreet, and its owners were friends of Sal and Nick from way back. They'd struck up a deal to provide B&M with rooms for ESA calls at a discount, and they valued discretion as much as Sal and Nick did.

There were even a handful of parking spaces reserved for ESAs attending calls in the hotel's underground garage. I gratefully slid my Ranger into one of those places. I hated getting into a boiling hot truck after a call, when I was already overheated from days of absorbing omega hormones, and even though it wasn't the middle of summer yet, the sun was hot enough.

I got out, slung my overnight bag and the ESA heat kit I'd picked up at B&M's mountain compound before leaving for the call over one shoulder, then locked my truck and started for the back entrance to the lobby, already running through not only the protocols for the call, but details of next week's trip as I walked.

I smelled the omega before I saw him. There was no scent on earth as delicious as an omega in heat. Ten years of going on multiple heat calls a month, and that first whiff of the client never got old.

This one was particularly strong, unusually so. The scent was like a lollipop. Not just any lollipop either. I was hit so hard with the memory of the gigantic lollipop my dad had bought for me on a family trip to the beach when I was eight —a lollipop that was bigger than my head and that I hadn't been able to make a dent in, let alone finish, even though I'd spent all day licking it—that I stopped for a second just to breath the scent in. My cock twitched hard, and if not for the tight restraint of my jeans, I would have instantly looked obscene.

But there was something else...off about the scent. Not to mention it was so strong that it was all around me and seeping into my pores, but I couldn't see another soul, let alone an omega, anywhere. An omega scent usually only got that strong after heat had already started. Sure, an omega's scent started to increase within a week of their heat starting, which was one way they knew it was coming, but it wasn't usually *that* strong until—

I spotted him as I stepped through the first of the lobby's two doors. The scent in the small, enclosed area between the two doors was so overpowering that I let out a low, alpha growl before I could stop himself. My dick filled so hard that, if I hadn't known better, I would have said I was in danger of knotting without even being in an omega.

But that was all irrelevant the moment my gaze landed on the small, lithe omega huddled into the fetal position in the corner of the vestibule, shaking like a leaf.

"Shit," I growled, moving faster as I approached the

omega. I crouched beside the man, dropping my bag and kit, and reached out a hand to gently move the hood of the omega's hoodie back.

The man was young, definitely a college kid. He had thick, black hair that stuck out in every direction, which might have been the fault of the hood that he'd been hiding in. His skin was smooth and pale, like a lot of omegas, and he had the most gorgeous, full lips. I immediately envisioned them wrapped around my cock as I sank deep into the omega's throat.

I sucked in a breath and shook the fantasy away. It was a typical, hormonal reaction and not to be taken seriously. What did need to be taken seriously was the state the omega was in.

"Mr. Curry?" I asked.

The omega gave no response. He seemed to shake harder, now that I was close to him, and if I wasn't mistaken, the seat of the man's jeans was soaking wet.

There was no time for polite introductions. "I've got you, Mr. Curry," I said in the soothing voice I'd practiced for the last decade. "No need to worry. I'm here now, and we'll work through your heat together. It's going to be alright."

I reached over to hoist my bag and heat kit over my shoulder again, then scooped the omega into my arms. Omegas were naturally smaller and lighter than alphas and betas. I was able to lift Mr. Curry as if he weighed nothing.

Mr. Curry moaned as if the gesture caused him pain when I stood. It was likely the unique sort of pain omegas felt when they had gone for hours into their heat without any relief from an alpha, or even toys. The sensation had once been described to me as the sort of whole-body pain that was felt when someone had a kidney stone. I'd never had one, but that didn't mean I wouldn't take Mr. Curry's pain absolutely seriously and get him up to a room as quickly as possible.

"You're going to be alright, Mr. Curry," I repeated, carrying the omega into the hotel lobby. "I've got you now."

Mr. Curry groaned again, clutching at my shirt and burying his face into the crook of my neck. He drew in several long breaths of my alpha scent, which only made him moan more, then closed his mouth over the small bit of exposed skin at my collar, licking and sucking as though he could get what he needed that way.

It felt so damn good. My alpha instincts roared to life so hard that I nearly missed a step as I headed to the end of the lobby desk, where priority check-in was located.

Want to know what happens next? Pick up *The Wrong Omega* here...

About the Author

I hope you have enjoyed *How to Train Your Alpha*. If you'd like to be the first to learn about when new books in the series come out and more, please sign up for my newsletter here: http://eepurl.com/cbaVMH And remember, Read it, Review it, Share it! For a complete list of works by Merry Farmer with links, please visit http://wp.me/P5ttjb-14F.

USA Today Bestselling Author Merry Farmer is an award-winning novelist who lives in suburban Philadelphia with her cats, Justine and Peter. She has been writing since she was ten years old and realized one day that she didn't have to wait for the teacher to assign a creative writing project to write something. It was the best day of her life. She then went on to earn not one but two degrees in History so that she would always have something to write about. Her books have reached the Top 100 at Amazon, iBooks, and Barnes & Noble, and have been named finalists in the prestigious RONE and Rom Com Reader's Crown awards.

Acknowledgments

I owe a huge debt of gratitude to my awesome beta-readers, Erica Montrose and Jolene Stewart, for their suggestions and advice. And double thanks to Julie Tague, for being a truly excellent editor and to Cindy Jackson for being an awesome assistant!

Click here for a complete list of other works by Merry Farmer.

Printed in Great Britain
by Amazon

23333680R00073